WE'LL NEVER HAVE PARIS

PARIS, JE T'AIME

ADRIANA ANDERS

To Miss Clara, Dave, Maz, Our Paulus, Shep, and Trix.
Forever and always, The Best Ones.

CHAPTER ONE

*C*olin

    If I hear that laugh one more time, I'll head up there, kick her door in, and…

I don't know. Something tough and mean. Something she'll remember for a very long time.

The fact that I can't come up with anything besides shoving her against the door and putting my mouth to hers is just a testament to how tired I am.

"Please shut up." I mutter under my breath, turning over and shoving my pillow over my head. "Shut up, shut up, shut up, you bloody…*American*."

Another laugh, this one more of a throaty guffaw than a giggle. It hits low in my abdomen and makes me want to turn all of this aggression outward. My hands tighten on the pillow and twist until I'm afraid I'll tear the sodding thing apart.

"All right!" she screeches, as loud as the pigeons in the bloody courtyard. "Talk soon, okay? Yeah, hun. I'll call. Yep."

Thank God. It's almost over.

Except that it isn't, of course.

Why do I always fall for the trap of thinking it's over when she's still got thirty minutes of nattering left? Every fucking weekend, she talks and talks and talks on the phone, at this ungodly hour. And every weekend, it takes an additional lifetime before she ends the call.

I'm sure she's talking to a bloke, with all the *sweethearts* and *honeys* and *pumpkins*. Which is a ludicrous thing to call a human being, by the way. *Pumpkin?* As an endearment? Might as well call the poor bugger rutabaga or potato, for fuck's sake. Sure are looking great today, my lovely little asparagus.

Even when she's not on the phone, she hums and sings and whistles and she's *always* off-key.

I go still and listen.

Not a sound. Oh, thank God. Blessed quiet, finally.

I yawn and stretch, pull the pillow away and relax after a moment's silence. Is today the day I'll get enough sleep? The day I won't walk into the pub feeling like a dried out turd. The day I'll look out my window and see Paris, a city of beauty and light, instead of the stinking, flat, grey place it's become.

Snuggling in, I relax and allow my mind to wander, images of the first time I saw the American easing into my conscious brain.

Perhaps three or four months back—an unseasonably hot day, I recall—I was checking my letterbox, my back to the building's front door, when it buzzed and swung open, letting in the sounds and smells of the street. There was a bang and a hiss and possibly the scent of sulfur. I should have known right then not to engage, not even to make eye contact. I should have gone straight up and locked my door. Or packed up my things and left town forever.

Sadly, given that I own my flat, along with the pub downstairs, that wasn't an option.

Instead of all the things I could have done to avoid coming into contact with the lush little blue-eyed monster, I made the mistake of turning.

She stood, humming under her breath, her pleasantly round silhouette framed in the doorway, like some sort of demonic, frilly fairy cake, looking innocent and lost and sweet, and releasing, like Beelzebub's brimstone, her own signature scent into the air. Only, instead of the blazing fires of hell, she smelled like sugar and bloody spice.

"Oh, bonjour," she said in what was, I'll admit, an all right accent for a Yank. If a little loud and excitable and bouncy.

I nodded and waited for her to slowly pass, all the while humming under her breath and dragging an enormous, shiny turquoise suitcase behind her. The damn thing was covered in sparkly stickers.

But it was the skirt that got me into trouble—or the dress, rather. The perfect poofy, flouncy equivalent to the mouth-watering scent that preceded her. It was nipped in at the waist, strained at the chest, and short enough to give a hint of what I'll admit is an unbelievably shapely pair of thighs, not to mention the arse above them. Round and wide and high enough to set a pint of lager on.

I was picturing just that when she turned and caught me looking.

The way she blinked—as if thoroughly shocked—seemed a bit absurd, given that the woman *had* to know the effect she had in that dress. Honestly, you don't wear something that bright or frilly or fitted with the expectation of being ignored, do you? No. No, I don't think so. It's illogical.

So, when she muttered, "Keep it in your pants, mister," under her breath, clearly thinking I wouldn't understand, I grinned and asked, "What pants, love?" to which she took issue.

Her mouth dropped open, those plump cheeks went from a pale rose to a dark pink and then her eyes—blimey, those eyes, two massive blueberry saucers—lowered to take in my crotch before rising to meet mine again.

"You are wearing pants," she said.

"Am I?" I'll admit, it was not my best moment. But she rubbed me the wrong way. Even then, before all the stomping and the early morning laughing and the *Punkins* and *Honeys*, some part of me knew the woman was trouble with a capital L for Lucifer.

Have you seen those pinup paintings from the 1940s? The ones where some adorably clueless bird bends to pick a flower and accidentally drops her knickers in the process? That's this girl. She's little and buxom and wide-eyed and looks like a walking, talking Norman Rockwell illustration. Not a real person at all.

Not to be trusted.

"You're English," she said, to which I replied that no,

I was in fact Welsh. I didn't mention the half French part. Wasn't her business, was it?

"Oh. Okay. Well. Bonne journée, sir," she said, pink-painted lips parting in a perfect, white smile, before she turned with a swish of mahogany hair and a sugary cloud of honey or vanilla or whatever pixy dust perfume her pores emit instead of regular human body odor.

Feigning interest in a piece of junk mail, I watched her lug her massive suitcase—along with a half a dozen smaller bags—past the lift. She stopped at the bottom of the steep, winding staircase, put a tiny, surprisingly unadorned hand on the railing, and looked up.

"What floor?" I asked.

She glanced over her shoulder at me, eyes narrowed. "Why do you want to know?"

I looked down at her case, which must have weighed a good thirty kilos, glanced at the lift door, and let my gaze return to her. "No reason at all." I gave her a quick, friendly smile on my way out. "Bonne journée to you, then."

Why the hell was I such an absolute git? I couldn't say. Some instinct, I suppose, telling me that the woman would make my life miserable.

And how right it was. Just as guilt rises up at the memory, the laughing starts again, jolting me out of that liminal place between waking and slumber.

Three months I've had to suffer through this. Three bloody months.

Rather than lie here and endure one more minute of

it, I force myself to roll out of bed and throw on a pair of tracksuit bottoms.

That's it.

We're nipping this in the bud. Now.

* * *

Jules

Uh oh. The second I hear the footsteps stomping up to my floor, I know it's him—Monsieur Grumpy Puss. Le neighbor from hell. The man who, for reasons entirely unknown to me, has hated me since the moment we met in the lobby.

He was the very first person I met in Paris. Not a good sign, if I were a superstitious sort of person.

Thankfully, I'm not, because Paris has turned out to be my favorite place. The people, the flutter of excitement every time I walk out the door, my job. Even the streets' very specific pastry, perfume, and exhaust smell speaks to something in my soul. Which makes my downstairs neighbor the only sour note in a truly memorable stay.

Solène warned me about this guy when she rented me the apartment, so I know it's not just me—although it sure feels like it sometimes.

The man on Floor 5 is difficult, but harmless. It's literally written out in Solène's arrival instructions. *Ignore him and he'll ignore you. He hates everyone. Keep the noise down and he'll leave you be.*

And I've done that. I have! I don't play music out loud, ever. I walk as lightly as I can. Always barefoot.

And I try to whisper through most of my calls. But he's hated me since the moment we met. How many times has he stopped me in the stairs or the front hall or come up to complain? Five? Six?

Honestly, it feels personal.

As he nears, I can feel his disapproval through the thick wooden front door and, for reasons I cannot explain, it revs me up, the way it has every time he's stomped up here.

Okay, so maybe I can explain it. Because yes he's an obnoxious, egotistical ass with questionable taste in music—which I sometimes hear and have never once complained about!—but he's shockingly, disgustingly attractive.

Which is so totally unfair.

Why, oh why are the hot ones always assholes?

And this one takes the cake. In both areas. Unbearably attractive and unfathomably crappy.

So, of course he's got a problem with me.

"I gotta go," I hiss at the screen.

"Is it him again? Le Jerk?" Nana stage whispers back. Over my past five months here, our calls have taken on the quiet, hurried, guilt-infused feel of sessions in the confessional. It would be funny if it weren't so annoying.

"Yep. Better face the music!" I can't explain the hint of glee in my voice.

"Don't hang up yet. Let me look at him. Give him a piece of my mind."

"No, Nana, I can't risk it. You'll go into cardiac arrest

the moment you see his ugly mug." I don't know why I keep down-playing the man's looks.

"Tell him what a woman my age can do to little boys who bully and fat-shame their beautiful, smart, hard-working, gorgeous, amazingly kind and—"

"Okay, Nana." I roll my eyes. "It's fine. You don't need to—"

He's pounding at the door. The entire floor shakes with it. In all fairness, the wood floor's such a mess it shakes if you sneeze in this place, but given that I'm paying almost no rent here, I can't complain.

I'll leave that to Le Grumpy Jackass. Or, in this case, Jacques-Ass.

"What the tarnation is he doing?" yells Nana, craning her neck as if she'll see better that way. "Is he trying to break the door down? You tell him—"

"Love you, Nana. Bye!"

I end the call, take a deep breath, and stalk to the door.

Then, because he may be rude, but that doesn't mean I have to be, I take a deep, calming breath and paste a curious and, hopefully, friendly smile on my face.

Slowly, carefully, I turn the three locks, one at a time, ease open the door, and use every bit of my willpower to stand my ground at the sight of him.

Because he's gorgeous, yes: dark and brooding, with wide, rounded shoulders I easily picture myself digging my nails into, messy, soft-looking brown hair I can just feel between my fingers, and a constant five o'clock shadow I imagine scraping the insides of my thighs. But the man is dangerous, too, and at this moment, angry as a hornet.

Also, he's shirtless and wearing low-slung, leave nothing to the imagination sweats. I can't look. I won't.

"Hey there, neighbor," I say in the voice I used when I worked at that daycare center in Lima. It's a calm, soothing voice. A kind voice, geared towards hyper kids and overbearing parents alike. Darn it, though. It's awful hard to keep my eyes above that angular clavicle and the scattering of wiry-looking hair below it. "Something wrong?"

"Yes, something's wrong." I spend way too much running over his accent in my head. Over and over. "I can't sleep."

"I'm sorry to hear that." I do my best to placate. I really do. I mean, he's not scary per se, but he is big and muscular and breathing fire, so it's definitely the smart thing to do.

Don't look down. Don't do it. And don't imagine that voice calling you a dirty girl and telling you to kneel and—

Oh geez, what is it about this guy that makes me like this? Yes, I'm attracted to the occasional man, but this level of physical interest is excessive.

Though I try my hardest not to notice, my peripheral vision gives me a healthy serving of dark curls, two thick, ridiculously defined pecs and…oh, crap. The abs, the happy trail, the…

He clears his throat and I blink back to reality.

"You need to keep your voice down."

"My *voice*?" I blink up at him, a little dizzy from my proximity to all this skin.

"On the phone. You're too damn loud."

"Am I? Oh, God. I'm so sorry." Okay, he's right. I can be loud. And the floors are paper thin. That said, "I've been whispering!"

"It's your laugh." My laugh? Oh, that lands low and hard, way below the belt. "It's so bloody…"

"What's wrong with the way I laugh?" Despite my effort to sound strong and self-assured, hurt seeps into my voice.

"Annoying."

Ooof. Okay.

But wait, people *like* my laugh. They say it's catching. They try to get me going just so they can hear it and laugh with me. Or at me or whatever. I don't mind either way.

There's this old man who comes to the chocolate shop every morning for the express purpose of getting me to laugh. Monsieur Astruc in his bowtie and jacket shuffles into the shop, slow, his back bent nearly double and buys a tiny box of pistachio macarons, then tells the same joke every morning. And every morning, I giggle. I can't help it. He's delightful.

So, for reasons I only half understand, it somehow actually hurts that ole' Grumpo here comes up and tears apart one thing about me that I know for a fact isn't awful. It feels personal and mean and…

Hold on. This isn't about me and my laugh at all, is it? I do everything I can to keep the volume down when I'm in the apartment. I take off my shoes the second I get in, whisper on the phone, and sit as soon as I can. Anything to keep him from pounding on the ceiling of

10

his apartment. No, no. This is about him being fat-phobic and misogynistic. The man's acted like garbage since I called him out for scowling at my ass my very first day in Paris.

He's got a thing against women, at least women who look like me.

Sure, it's a big butt. Get over it! If I've got no problem with the size of my behind, I don't see how he can possibly find it offensive. It's a *butt*, for crying out. The butt I was born with. The fact that people—okay, *men*—think it's okay to judge and leer and make all kinds of unsolicited, sizeist comments about my body is astounding to me.

So, yeah, forgive me if I ignore his nonsense complaints and objectify Le Jerk for a moment. He's clearly okay with that kind of thing.

The way he's glaring down at me now, like he'd burn holes through me with those eyes if he could, just reinforces my belief that this is about more than just an early morning noise complaint.

This is his problem, not mine. The man wants war? Well, maybe it's time I gave it to him.

Sucking in a deep, steadying breath, I rack my brain for something that'll take him down a peg. Something big, huge. A single phrase that will cut him to the quick.

Without thinking it through, I open my mouth and ask, "Have you considered calling the Guinness Book people?"

Oh no. What am I doing?

A moment of silence and then, "What?"

11

"You're, like, the angriest man on earth or something."

"I'm *not*." How can he possibly sound so surprised? Offended. He has to have an inkling of how grumpy he is.

"You're literally telling me not to *laugh*. Who does that?"

His scowl deepens. "Your cackling keeps me up."

Cackling? It shouldn't bug me that he says this. It shouldn't, but it does, a little. "That's the building's fault, not mine."

"How so?" The landing's worn wood floor creaks under his feet.

Everything in this building scrapes and ticks and drips and creaks. Even when it's quiet, it's loud. At night, I hear the elevator's high-pitched squeal from my bed, which is behind two walls. From up here on the 6th —and last—floor, I can tell when Madame Christen on two takes her tiny dog for a walk by the tinkling of its collar. Sure, he lives right below me, but even so, the fact that he can isolate my voice from the cacophony is almost unbelievable.

"I hear you moving around, too, you know. And you're right under me."

Under me. Crap. Why does that sound so sexual?

"You hear *me*?" His dark eyes narrow. "I doubt that."

I shake my head, kind of shocked at how awful he is. "Oh, you don't believe me? Great. Well, let's see. There was *Scarface* last Monday. Right?"

He jolts like I've hit him. "How can you possibly know that?"

"You're not *listening* to me. Pay attention, big guy. I *heard* it," I tell him. "Every word."

"Oh, really?" He folds insanely thick arms over his chest and leans against my doorframe, giving my ratty T-shirt and shorts a quick, dismissive up and down look. "Give me one line," he says in the exact tone of voice I imagine him telling me to open my mouth and—

Oh my God, shut it down. Shut it down, Jules!

"One? Okay." I focus back in. "How about, *Say hello to my little friend*. At the end, when he mows down a bunch of guys. Or, hey. I've got another." I launch into a pretty decent Al Pacino imitation. "*I'm Tony Montana! You eff with me, you effin' with the best.*"

It's possible a shadow of a smile crosses his face. Although, it's probably an angry tick pulling at his mouth. Totally involuntary. I'd be willing to bet his lips haven't seen anything resembling humor in a decade.

"All right, then." He shifts against the doorframe, like he's settling in for the long haul, nearly filling it in the process. "What did I watch Sunday?"

"Sunday?" I consider for a few seconds. "Trick question." I feel a thrill of triumph as I step closer. "You weren't *here* Sunday."

"Hm," is his only response and, for reasons I can't explain, it infuriates me, but it also makes me pay closer attention to that mouth and, let me tell you about the man's mouth. It's sort of lush when he's not sneering. And sort of pouty in a way that doesn't go with the rest of him. At all. It doesn't curve up, but when he's not actively being hateful, it's maybe...sweet-looking? Almost. "Last week?"

13

"The Thing." I'm enjoying the way his irritation grows with every correct answer I throw out. "Oh, *Inception*, too. That's a good one. Before then, let's see." I tick them off on my fingers as I go. *"Die Hard. Speed!* One and two, which is a questionable choice. One's a classic. Without Keanu, Two is... You know what? I could go on, but I've got better things to do." Like shower, get dressed, go to work, serve chocolates to delightful little elderly men who like the way I laugh.

"Good." He bends until his face is almost level with mine and his voice comes out low and menacing. "Do them quietly."

Or what? I just barely refrain from asking. He's close enough that I feel the heat from his breath, the tension in his half-clothed body. The cold air coming up the stairs has turned my nipples into two sharp points that he'd definitely notice if he looked down.

My breathing's shaky, my body buzzing from this confrontation like I've run up all six flights—or lugged my suitcase up them, the way I did that first day. When the jerk somehow forgot to mention that there was a perfectly good—if tiny—elevator right there for me to use.

Okay, good is an exaggeration, but at least the thing works. Most of the time. Well, occasionally.

Any normal person would've stopped me and pointed it out. But not Le Jerk. Oh, no, he's way too brooding and angry for that. He's the kind of misogynistic jackass who probably feeds on the blood of puppies, cancels Christmas for kids, and pipes the sounds of crying babies into his earbuds to get to sleep

14

at night. Watching a woman struggle up half a dozen floors with a five-ton suitcase is probably just a mise en bouche.

I mean, what kind of assface stomps upstairs at 5 a.m. on Christmas Eve to complain about someone's laugh, for God's sake? I drag in a deep breath, hating how his warm, sleepy smell curls low in my belly. "You know what you are?"

His gaze skates down—to my lips? To my breasts?—and I swear he grows an extra inch or two. "What am I?"

"Well, it's…" I pretend to look at a watch that doesn't exist. "Oh, look, the day before Christmas and you're up here, the sad, lonely old guy with—"

"Old?"

Ignoring him, I carry on, my pulse quickening as I go. "—nothing better to do than harass your neighbor. So I guess that makes you just like Ebeneezer Scrooge, doesn't it?"

His face goes dark and thunderous as he bends closer, bringing us, for a weird, breathless second, dangerously close to kissing distance. Suddenly, all that cold, angry animosity heats the air between us and I wonder, has this all just been foreplay? Has every second of this exchange, from the moment he stomped up here in nothing but those loose, low-slung joggers led to this moment? Is this some messed-up, Grinchy, British version of first base?

I swear he's as nervous or aware or excited as I am when he tilts his head and starts to shift that last inch, just as I press up to my tiptoes to meet him, closer, closer, until—

15

"Hé ho!" We jump apart. "Putain, ca va, oui!" someone yells from a few floors down. It's Madame Christen, the elderly woman on floor two, with the tiny dog and the one shoe taller than the other. She complains constantly. "On essaye de dormir là," she shrieks, which I guess I can't blame her for, given that it is very early on Christmas Eve and people *should* be able to sleep in.

Another door opens and a man's voice calls out, with humor, rather than anger, "Ouais! Il y a des hôtels pour ça." It takes me a second to realize it's the French equivalent of someone shouting, *Get a room!*

I gasp and the grump steps back onto the landing, his eyes wide and shocked for a split second before his features settle into his usual resting jerk face.

"Just...keep it down." He gives me a final blue-eyed glare and spins toward the stairs.

Being my usual mature self, I search for something to say before he's gone, open my mouth and hiss, "No, *you* keep it down."

I'm good at comebacks like that.

CHAPTER TWO

*C*olin
        Owning a pub in the center of Paris isn't quite the dream it's cracked up to be. It's exhausting and sometimes depressing and often confrontational. Don't get me wrong—I like my punters, mostly. But I'll admit there are times when being nice to people who come in and order a coffee and water and sit there all night, taking up table space and spending absolutely nothing, is a challenge.

"All right, Stevie, ready for another?" I ask one of my regulars in English, eyeing his empty pint glass.

"Nah, best be off. The mister made a roast and veg. We've got his parents coming in for the day."

I grunt in response, which usually keeps people from going on too long.

"His dad's a wanker." Sadly, Stevie ignores my nonverbal signals. "But I've got to be there or he'll have my balls."

I give another grunt, relieved as always that I've got

no one to answer to, no one to hurry home for. No pressure to perform or smile or be nice on a day like today.

Today being Christmas. Well, almost. And nothing good comes at Christmas.

Which is why I'm sipping whisky behind the bar, wishing for a crowd to distract me. Crowds are good, even if the people are mostly arseholes. Crowds keep my hands busy and my mind off of everything else.

Stevie slaps a twenty on the bar.

I nod my thanks and he takes off, leaving me alone.

Shit. Got nothing to do now, have I? The place has been scrubbed and polished to a shine, the floors are freshly mopped, the booze restocked. The loo's clean and ready for the next onslaught of punters.

Which won't be tonight.

Something knocks at the door and I look up only to see an empty coffee cup caught in an eddy of wind, knocking at the glass like a ghost of Christmas past. Like regret.

Stupid paper coffee cup. Paris has finally fallen to the carry-out coffee craze, direct from the States, which is not a good thing.

Mention of the States makes me think of my neighbor. Of course it does.

How could I not think of her when she's responsible for today's exhaustion? Not to mention the constant half hard-on.

I sigh and look down. I could give up, I suppose. Let the fire die out, grab a bottle and head upstairs for a wank and a film. Something loud and aggressive and old school that will *really* get her back up. *Rocky* or *Rambo*. She'd hate *Rambo*, wouldn't she?

Well, perhaps not. She knew lines from *Scarface*, which I'll admit surprised me. The woman looks like a walking lolli, so the idea that she might be a fan of grim, vintage mafia movies seems like cognitive dissonance. Perhaps a horror film would be better, to cover whatever off-key singing she does.

I grin, considering. I could do the full *Purge* series, couldn't I? Keep her up late with the screaming.

Fuck. Why on earth did I just go and think of late-night screaming? Because, yes, I'd meant it in a violent, bloody way, but my libido immediately feeds me a more pleasurable version—her beneath me, those massive tits out in the open, nipples as hard as they were under that ridiculous little T-shirt this morning, her back arched and me balls deep inside a body I think about *constantly*. I think of that sweet scent she walks around with. Some vanilla or spice or chocolate. I don't bloody know, do I? What I know is that if her smell haunts me from a distance, I suspect that if I got close and put my face between her legs, it would be absolute hea—

Damn it!

Another knock against the door draws my attention with a start. I must look as guilty as when twelve-year-old me discovered that Mrs. Arbonaut forgot to close her bedroom shades at the weekend, which led me to make up every possible excuse to sit by my window and wait for that magical moment when the bra came off.

The face looking in, however, isn't close to Mrs. Arbonaut's, with her tight little blonde bun and that bright red lippy she wore every single day. No, this face is long and gaunt, the nose broken a time or two, the smile as crooked as the rest of him.

I look up and the man pushes inside, glancing about to ensure we're alone. "Y'a personne?"

"Yep. Nobody here, Raf." I shake my head. "Looks windy out there. Cold."

He nods and smiles and slaps his gloved hands together for warmth.

"Fire's lit," I tell him. It's as close to an invitation as he'll get. I pull a carton from the refrigerator, take off the top, and slide it into the microwave. "Duck?"

"Mais non," he protests, waving me away as he starts to turn back towards the door. It's his usual dance and I let him get a couple meters away before calling him back.

"My friend ordered it at lunch. Something came up and he had to leave before it arrived." A bald-faced lie. "Mine's upstairs. This will go to waste if you don't eat it."

The oven dings and he walks over, drops his bag and settles at the bar. I draw him a pint of bitter and pour one for myself, ignoring the smoke and body odor smell coming off him. "All right, Raf. You been home at all this week?"

"Nah. Too much work." His tone is fatalistic, uncon-cerned. "It would take me hours on the RER and then I'd just have to turn around and come back."

"Welcome to run up to mine if you need a kip."

Shaking his head, he slurps down half the beer and smacks his lips.

"It's Christmas," I remind him, as if the lights and decorations and frantic last-minute shoppers haven't made that obvious enough. "You could celebrate with a nap and a shower."

"Ouais." With a wide smile, he accepts the plate of food and the cloth napkin and cutlery, eyes the empty bar in front of me, and, after I nod to him to go ahead, tucks in. "I need to be out there." He takes a bite of duck breast and leans back with a sigh. "Best night of the year for chestnuts."

Chestnuts, which he roasts over a barrel fire just up the way and sells to passersby wrapped in day-old newspaper. In the summer, he hawks sweet-scented jasmine wreaths and roses to tourists sitting at outdoor tables, which is a more dangerous job than you'd think. Between getting run off by annoyed restaurateurs, yelled at by couples in the midst of break-ups, and accused of all kinds of crap, including stealing a woman's necklace off her person—who it turned out had taken it off back at her hotel and forgot, the silly cow—the man deserves hazard pay.

Also, he saved my arse once when a couple of drunk geezers came in and tried to hold me up at closing. One of the bastards had just thrown a full pint in my face—glass and all—when Raf showed up and kicked him right in the bollocks.

The wind rattles the door. Someone scurries by beyond the plate glass windows. In the corner, the fire sputters in the wood-burner. "It's cold."

"All the better," he says with a grin. "I'm raking it in today." He wiggles his fingers before diving back into

21

his meal with the sort of gusto I've not felt in ages. For anything, really. Well, that's not entirely true. I was pretty fucking motivated this morning when it came to putting my annoying little neighbor in her place. Although I wouldn't call it gusto so much as pure irritation.

Raf finishes up. I clear his plate, pull out the bûche de Noël I bought from the little chocolate place on the square. It's a hazelnut log, frosted with dark chocolate and decorated with little marzipan and meringue mushrooms.

"Ah, non, c'est trop, Colin. J'peux pas." He tries to refuse, but I shove the box at him anyway.

"C'est Noël, Raf. Go on. I won't eat it. Don't make me throw it in the bin."

The look he gives me is grudging and embarrassed.

"You suddenly celebrate Christmas now?" he asks.

I grunt, watching as he opens the box and eyes the frosted yule log with hunger and excitement and an edge of resignation that I feel to my toes.

The pastry, he decides, is for later. Now, while the occasional tourist or other straggler is still about, he's got work to do. Chestnuts to roast and sell.

I walk him to the door and hand him a hot coffee— in a thick porcelain mug—laced with Irish whiskey. He accepts it, shaking his head like I've annoyed him, then turns to go. "Close up and go home, Colin." He looks at the blustery square, though I feel his side-eye. "You look like hell." Outside, he turns and flashes me a grin before stomping over to where he's stashed his still-smoking grill.

Shaking my head, I watch him go, wishing I felt the kind of lightness he carries inside him.

Another hard gust of wind rattles the windows, this time bringing with it a spatter of rain.

Yes, I should go. No point staying here in weather like this, on a night like this.

Fucking Christmas.

Quickly, now that I've made my decision, I close the damper on the fireplace insert, turn out the lights, grab the money bag and my coat and, after some hesitation, a full bottle of whisky, then head out into the cold.

CHAPTER THREE

*J*ules

"I'm fine, Nana. I promise."

"But, Sugar, you're all alone."

"I'm not alone!" I insist. "I'm in a building full of people." I'm not sure this is strictly true, given how quiet it's been all evening. Enora, my friend and sixth floor neighbor, took off for her boyfriend's parents' alpine ski lodge last night. Laurent, whose ground floor antique shop is usually aglow with old-fashioned lighting and the cozy *chug chug* of tiny trains, left to stay with his sister in Alsace and, when I rolled in exhausted from work earlier, the whole place just felt silent as a tomb. Still, empty, lifeless. Even Le Grump seems to have taken off for the holidays given how quiet he's been all night. At least I can laugh freely now.

Somehow, the thought doesn't pep me up like it should.

"You should've come home." Nana works hard to be heard over the sloppily merry sounds of a dozen retirees caroling under the influence of one too many heavily-laced veg nogs. They're just getting started. It's lunchtime on the West Coast.

"Too expensive." Which is only part of it, but Nana knows how I feel about where I grew up.

"I'd have helped out," she yells and then, seemingly as one, the entire vocal power of the Bellingham Bells golden age gay and lesbian choir pitches in with their *Yeahs!* and *Me, toos* and *It's not too late, honeys*, but it is too late.

And the thing I've never quite admitted to Nana or to the rest of my family is that I don't ever want to go back there. Visits—even short ones—take too much out of me, every time.

"I know, Nana," I tell her with a smile. "By the time I made it to you, I'd have had to turn around anyway."

"Don't they give you time off in that place?"

I sigh, sinking back onto the soft sofa. "Yes. I told you. This is France. I'd get five weeks if I had a permanent contract."

"Five! Good lord. And they couldn't have—"

"Nana," I interrupt, too drained to argue again—especially given that there's no point. I'm here for Christmas and then traveling south. To Italy next. Then, who knows? Maybe Greece. I only spent a couple weeks in the Cyclades last time.

This is what I do. I travel. I work. I stay with friends or rent cheap digs and then move on when my visa expires or whoever I'm crashing with gets sick of me. So, when Solène, my exchange student friend from back in high school, offered up her Paris apartment for three months in exchange for utilities and some plant watering, I jumped at the chance. Who wouldn't, right?

Of every place I've been since I took off at eighteen —and there have been many—Paris is my favorite. I feel alive here, like every time I step outside, there's an adventure waiting. But also weirdly at home? It's not just the city, either. My job—a fluke, last minute replacement—has me happy to get up in the morning. Sure, it's all paid under the table, which sometimes makes me feel in some ways like I don't really exist. But this apartment is bliss. I love it, with its brightly colored walls, its cozy furnishings, the huge windows and tiny balcony overlooking the sweetest, most picturesque pedestrian square, and beyond it, rooftops upon rooftops.

I just wish…

"I know, baby." Nana lets out a theatrical sigh. "You'll rest when you're dead."

My life motto. The rules I've lived by for almost ten years now. "Exactly," I say, not sounding nearly as cheery as I'd like. "Can't stop, won't stop," I add, just to make sure she buys it. Even if it's starting to sound old, even to me.

"Aren't you off to Italy soon?"

"Yes!" I smile wide, overcompensating for the hollow feeling inside. "You know how it is!"

"I do." She inspects me with sharp eyes, the sound of merriment around her somehow highlighting how quiet my own Christmas Eve is. Nana knows how much I hate silence. "Paris seems to suit you, though. Don't you want to try to get that visa thing and stay?"

I wish. I really do. But at the same time, the idea scares me. Staying still scares me.

"I'm gonna go, okay?" I swallow back a sudden wave of panic.

"What for?" She accepts my change of subject, though I can see how badly she wants to press. "You got some hot guy waiting in the wings?"

Yeah, right. I snort, my brain going straight to Le Jerk and his specific brand of annoying, angry hotness.

"I'm tired. I told you, we've been slammed at the shop and I've got to pack up and leave. I need to sleep." And finish this bottle of wine. And maybe bake something, because why the hell not? I haven't made eggnog yet this year. Oh, and maybe I'll put on high heels and dance, since mean old neighbor's not around. Although I'd maybe dance even if he were here, just to see what he'd do. To get him riled up, maybe send him running up here in nothing but boxers this time. Which, of course, makes me wonder, not for the first time, if he even wears them.

Darn it. Here I go again. I *hate* how often I think about that pants comment he made my first day here. Pants, I'd forgotten, refers to underwear in the UK, which insinuates the guy goes around commando. Since that first meeting—and literally every time I've seen him these past three months—that no pants comment's been hanging above my head like a big, perverted question mark.

After we say our goodbyes, I end the call and, before the silence can settle in, head to the ornate wooden wardrobe that serves as my closet and pull out the sparkly rose gold slingbacks I bought the other day in a little vintage clothing shop down the street. They're impractical and ridiculous and they sort of cut off the circulation to my toes, but I don't care. I love everything about them, from the delicate spike heel to the sweet little bows at the tips. They're party shoes. Dancing shoes. Get your butt out there and shake it shoes.

Refilling my wine, I slip them on and walk the tiny living room floor up and back, up and back, with that perverse little rush I get whenever I even think about him down there.

I slurp more wine, letting it warm me to my scrunched-up toes, and head over to the minuscule kitchen area, wondering if he's at home down there and if so, what he's doing and if he'll—

I open the fridge, get hit by the stink of the century, and gag.

Ew, oh my *God*. Argh. What *is* that smell?

I reach blindly for a dish towel, press it to my face, and search through the cold food remnants until I unearth a soft cheese I bought a while back and promptly forgot all about. Now, it's turned into a flat brown, crusty puddle in the crisper.

I almost vomit about twelve times while cleaning the nasty thing up, then get it into the trash, which I double bag and tie off in hopes that it'll keep until morning.

Not happening, though. No matter how many bags I put this thing in, it stinks to high heaven. I'll suffocate if I leave it here overnight. Death by cheese.

Ugh. Okay. Fine. I'll take it down.

I slug back the last of my glass, feeling a little buzzed

as I head to the door, still in my gorgeous heels, but you know what? Why not?

Everyone's left the building for the holidays. Hell, half the population's probably left Paris. I might as well enjoy the shoes, if only for myself.

So, buzzed and half-dressed, wobbling on my impractical dream shoes, I leave my overheated apartment, keys in my pocket and crusty old cheese bag hanging on the tip of my outstretched fingers, held as far in front of me as possible.

It feels like a Christmas miracle when I push the button and the elevator actually comes. I get in and push the RdC button for the ground floor and then waste what feels like a year of my life while it chugs its way down. It's not until the elevator does its weird third floor grind and lurch that it hits me just how cold it's gotten.

Earlier, I'd complained about the sad, warm drizzle and how I missed real cold weather. Suddenly, the building's an ice tunnel. And here I am in pajama shorts and a tank top, with nothing but a thin velour hoodie thrown over it, when what I need is one of those goose down parkas they give you when you move to Antarctica. Holy crap, it's *cold*.

As the elevator settles, I'd love to rush out, but I know better with this finicky little monster. Shivering now, I wait for it to finish making that slow, mechanical noise it lets out as it finally comes to a full stop, and then drag open the accordion doors, turn the handle and push the iron and glass outer door. In the half dark, I race back to the little trash area in the open-air courtyard, throw the bag into a can and shut the lid.

Above me, the light clicks on, which means someone's probably just come in through the main door. Huh. Okay. Not alone, I guess. It's a relief until I look down at myself.

What kind of dingdong heads out like this?

A cold one. That's what kind.

A huge gust of wind blows down into the courtyard and I scurry back toward the elevator and the stairs, which might not be fully enclosed, but also aren't out here in the frigid, wet outside. Whoever just came in will have to deal with the sight of me in my silly PJs.

If I'm lucky, it's a first-floor neighbor who's already halfway up the steps and I can avoid them entirely. Wrapping my arms around myself, I traipse over the cobbled stones and reenter the lobby just in time to see the elevator door swing closed.

"Tenez la porte!" I yell, hoping they'll hear me and hold the door. I really don't want to trudge up all six flights in these shoes. "J'arrive!"

Is that someone pressing a button in there? No. No way would anyone be so cruel as to refuse to hold the elevator, right?

I stretch for the door, my fingers graze the handle and, just when I think I won't make it, I latch on, twist, and...the door gives.

"Oh, merci," I gasp, so thankful, whether whoever's in here helped me or not, that I'm smiling hugely when I shove open the interior doors, and go stock still. "Crap."

It's my grumpy-ass neighbor, obviously. I mean, who

else would pull that kind of Grinch move on someone who's begging to get in?

And worst of all, he looks put out by my presence.

Well, whatever. I'm cold and my feet hurt and it's Christmas Eve, dammit. So just this once, he can deal with my presence.

I step inside, quickly turning to shut the folding doors as the outer one slams, enclosing me and Ebenezer in a space so small you can touch every wall while standing in the middle. With his hulking shape taking up more than half of the space, it's uncomfortably tight.

Please go. Just go, I silently beg the world's slowest elevator, while behind me, Le Jerk exudes his own special brand of silent malevolence.

If I just ignore him, maybe he won't find anything to complain about.

CHAPTER FOUR

$\mathcal{C}$olin
My brain shuts down the moment she steps inside, a voluptuous goddess dressed for the hottest of summer days. Good God. "What the hell are you wearing?" I spit out, unable to peel my gaze from those dainty little feet.

"Excuse me?" She turns, positively affronted.

But really, look at her. Her hair's a wild red bush sprouting from a knot at the top of her head and her body's encased in nothing but a pair of shorts in soft-looking, light blue fabric that's stretchy and skin-tight and leaves absolutely nothing to the imagination. She's wearing a hoodie that's got that ridiculous cartoon cat on it and, the crux of this whole look is those *shoes*. They're a light, rusty-looking pink with pointy toes and bows and heels about a meter high, which, though she's dressed casually, does something to her body. Makes her stand up straight, perhaps? Forces that round, ample chest forward, arches her back and thrusts that wide, plump arse in my direction.

"Fuck," I mutter, shutting my eyes against this unbearably bold display of American excess.

"What is wrong with you, Ebenezer? Seriously, just push the button and let me—"

"Close the doors," I order, my voice much too harsh, each word a sharply bitten-off demand. "There's a gap. We can't move if they're open."

What I really want to tell her is to get out and wait for me to send it back. Or, if she likes, she can take this one and I'll walk. I could use the exercise. My brain could use the oxygenated blood now that she's wedged herself into this narrow space and it's all flowed south.

"Oh. Oh, sorry." She turns back, her hip skimming my thigh in the process, and slams the two folding doors more tightly shut, which sets the elevator off on what is usually a slow climb. Right now, in such close quarters with this loud, living sex doll of a woman, it's a torturous slog.

She remains facing the door. Thank God. Slowly, I let the air out of my lungs, plaster my backside to the mirror, and shut my eyes against the sight of her.

Not that it's a bad sight. Just the opposite. My eyes slit open of their own volition. The way she looks hits me in places I've never before noticed. That arse, for example, with its deep dimples, makes my thighs clench with the desire to feel her weight on them. Her waist, little in comparison to the rest, but still thick, makes my fingers itch to sink in, knead, shape. And her nape—

fuck, I want to put my mouth there and bite down right at the hairline. Just to see her reaction. Just to feel the beating of her pulse, the thump of her heart beneath those luscious breasts. Maybe to get her to scream. See if she's as loud when she comes as she is when she laughs.

"What are you doing?" she asks over her shoulder.

I jolt. "What do you mean?"

"You're, I don't know, whispering or something? Muttering."

"No, I'm not."

"You are." She folds her arms over her chest, pushing them up and, from my position above and behind her, giving me a perfect view of soft-looking cleavage.

I tear my gaze away.

Through the cracks in the elevator's seams, I watch the first floor go by at a snail's pace.

"You imagined it."

She snorts. "Yeah. Like you imagined me laughing this morning."

"Oh, you laughed."

"Whatever, Ebenezer. Just quit muttering behind my back."

My breathing's gone fast and hard and my lungs feel tight. I've got the urge to tug her shoulder and turn her round, make her look at me and confront me to my face.

Which is ridiculous. I know this. I'm being absurd. And yet, I *want* it. And that feeling—of really craving something—is so foreign I've got no idea how to react. Maybe it's the whisky I started in on while locking up the pub, or the season or some other incomprehensible thing, but something pushes me to open my mouth. "You're being rude."

After a handful of silent seconds that feel like the calm before the storm, she swings halfway back to glare at me. Then she laughs. "Oh my God. What is wrong with you? You're like…" Her mouth snaps shut before she turns to the front again, shaking her head. "No. Nope. Not doing this. Not even a little bit. It's Christmas and I'm…" She inhales deeply, lifts her hands into the air and circles them with a graceful, almost dance-like movement. They're tiny hands. Short-fingered and plump, with neat, clean, unpainted nails. "Embodying the Christmas spirit. Even with Le Jerk."

"Le *what?*"

"Le Jerk. It's one of my many names for you."

"Many?" My brow wrinkles. "Such as?"

There's a moment of silence as the lift hitches, as usual, at the third floor then, after a shuddering pause, carries onward and upward.

"Oh, you know, like Grumpopotomus. Grumposaurus Rex, Grumpy McJerkyson, or—"

"I'm not a jerk, I'm just—"

She turns. "You're what? Kindness itself? Sweetness and light? No. No, sir, you're mean and you're a creep, who has always, from day one, treated me like—"

"A creep? Does that mean the same thing in your language? Because I've never—"

"My *language?*" One tiny index finger rises. I watch with fascination as it prods at my chest. "I speak *English* you jackwagon."

"No, you don't. You're American, which is—"

"Some say closer to the original old English than—"

"*What?* That's absurd. You talk like—"

The lift chooses that moment to start its slow, agonizing final grind to the fifth floor, for some strange reason, always slower and more laborious than the lower floors. "Never mind. We're here." Thank God. One, two. Another half-second and we've arrived. Impatient, I lean forward, work one arm around her and pull hard at the door.

The lift's lights go out.

"What the hell just happened?" she asks.

No. No, God no. *Please.*

I peer out through the crack behind her and see that we're probably thirty centimeters below the fifth floor landing. Why? How? I felt it arrive. I felt the easing, the final slowing, the bump and shift. No. No, this cannot be happening.

I push the fifth floor button. Nothing happens. No slow, ancient motor revving to life, no lights blinking back on. Nothing.

We're in a tiny metal cage hanging five stories in the air.

To make matters worse, the hallway lights choose that moment to turn off with a resonant clank, familiar but somehow louder than it's ever been.

Splendid. Wonderful.

I've said a million times that nothing good ever comes of this holiday. And yep, voilà, here we are, caught in the dark, *alone* with my sexy little nemesis.

Merry fucking Christmas to all.

CHAPTER FIVE

*J*ules

This can't be happening. It can't. Not me stuck with this hot grinch of a man, hanging six floors—not five, like the French would have you believe—above the ground in this creaky antique metal box, wearing my *freaking* party shoes and little else.

Please, God. Don't do this.

I shut my eyes and picture how warm it is in my apartment. Hot, even, because of some weird radiator thing. So hot, I wear summer PJs and open the bedroom window so I won't suffocate in my sleep. Of course, that won't be an issue now, since I'll freeze to death here instead.

"Push a button," I say, to my neighbor's obvious annoyance.

"What do you think I'm doing?"

"Nothing, as far as I can tell."

"I'm pushing buttons."

"Here, let me try." I turn in the dark, step on his toes, and bump into some part of him, which leads to more of that muttering he started a couple floors down, then bat his hand aside. "Do you even know which button it is?"

"Yes. I do." His voice is low and angry. "And it's not working."

"Okay, well, maybe if I turn my flashlight on—" Halfway through patting my pockets, I realize I left my phone upstairs. I've got my keys and nothing else. Well, besides the torture devices into which I chose to stuff my feet before heading out into the frigid night.

"You carry a flashlight?"

"The one on my phone." I sigh. "Which I left up in my place. You got yours?"

He scuffles around, to the sounds of crinkling paper. Seconds later, a phone screen lights up the too-dark, too-tight space.

Oh, thank God. That's better.

After a second's fumbling, he turns the flashlight toward the elevator buttons and presses the 5.

Nothing. No light, no movement. No century-old engine warming up.

"Try the six," I tell him, surprised when he actually obeys.

Nope.

"That one." I point at the red button engraved with a bell.

With what sounds like a sigh of relief, he pushes it. A harsh ringing shrieks through the building.

"Good," he says. "That's sure to wake up anyone who's sleeping."

I nod, full of hope, a little excitement. He smacks the button again and I swear the sound rattles the whole elevator shaft.

We wait, bodies tense, ears perked.

Again, he stabs at the damn thing and this time, I put my hands up to cover my ears. But still, there's not a sound from the rest of the building. Not a door opens. Not a voice, not a freaking footfall.

"Come on, please," I whisper. "Isn't there a call button? Like, a way to get the elevator people here?"

"The elevator people?" There's that tone of voice again. The one that's equal parts judgment, annoyance, and disbelief.

"You know. The emergency line."

He swings his light one way, then the other. "No. Nothing."

I'm shivering. From cold, from panic. I don't know. But the feeling's pretty close to hysteria. And I've known hysteria before. The bad, bad kind. The kind that keeps you from making sense and makes you hurt, inside and out. The kind that squeezes your lungs until you can't breathe and messes so badly with your brain it's never the same again.

"You've got to fix this, dude. Please. Please, just…"

"It's dude now, is it?" he asks in that low, sarcastic voice. As if we're not stuck here, just the two of us, in what's *clearly* an empty building on the quietest day of the year. "Not Jerk? Or Grumparino? Not Wankersaurus?"

"That's not what I called you." I manage to sound calm, but that inner voice is working its way up to a shriek.

"Close enough." His light goes out, which sets my pulse racing even harder. "I'll just call the pompiers round. Hold on."

"Oh, yes. Right. The firemen. Good." In Paris, if you need something done, you don't call the police or an ambulance, you call the pompiers. They resuscitate, scale buildings, put out fires. Everything, really. They'll get us out of here. They'll save us. The shrieking subsides.

In the dim light from the phone, his face is an eerie blue, but it's enough. Better than the pure dark from earlier. Something to stare at. Something to hold on to, along with the hope that we'll get out of here soon. I watch closely as he pokes at the screen.

"You all right?"

I look up from his mobile's cool glow to find him watching me. "What?"

"You're shivering."

"I'm...I'm...fine."

"Your teeth are chattering," he insists, as if I'm doing it specifically to annoy him.

"It's not from the cold." Now why did I tell him that? What good could it possibly do to admit to this man that I'm scared out of my wits right now?

"No?" Even in the minimal blue wash of light, I see the way his gaze flicks down to my feet before returning to my face. "That's a shocker."

"Just... Why aren't you calling?"

He sighs. "No service. As usual." The hand holding his phone drops to his side. "Fucking stone building."

"What about the emergency call thing? Try that?"

"I've tried. Nothing's going through."

"Give me that." With surprisingly little resistance, he hands me the phone and... Crap. No bars. Not one. To top it off, the battery's in the red. "You're at 3 percent?" What kind of monster lets their phone get that low?

"Jesus, woman. I didn't know I'd be stuck in a lift with a half-naked yank harpy, did I? I was heading up to mine after a painfully slow night at the pub, when you—"

"Oh, no you don't. No way do you blame me for getting us stuck in here. You're the one who opened the door prematurely. That's all on you, buddy. I'm just here, minding my own business."

"Half naked."

"Like I said, *minding my own business*, when you—"

"Why *are* you dressed like that, by the way?"

"Smelly cheese."

He snorts. "You went to the shop to buy cheese, when—"

"No! I found it in the fridge and had to throw it in the garbage and was headed back to my—"

"Did you touch it?"

"What?"

"Oh, thank God." The snuffling laugh he lets out makes me want to smack him. "It's a relief, actually. I'd thought you'd forgot to wash or something."

"Forgotten to..." Mortification floods through me on a hot, prickly wave. "Can you smell it?"

"Like feet, only worse."

"Oh, no." I sniff my hands, the air. "I got used to it, I guess."

"Right, well, it's a change from your normal smell."

I go rigid and all the hot blood that flooded my system a second ago just washes out. "My *what?*"

In the few uncomfortable seconds of complete silence that follow, I notice that we are once again surrounded by pitch black. I'm not panicked about it now, though. Oh no. Now, I'm too busy panicking about whatever this smell is that I apparently exude.

When he says, "Nothing," as if he hasn't just literally compared me to a stinky cheese, it takes every bit of my willpower to back down and pretend like it's nothing.

It's safer this way.

"We need to get out of here." I turn and mess with the folding doors for a few seconds, will them to open. "Allo!" I yell, my voice getting swallowed up by the space above and below us. "Au secours!"

"Il y a quelqu'un?" the jerk neighbor shouts, significantly louder. "Allo! Madame Christen? Laurent?"

"He's gone."

He bellows, "Enora!"

"Skiing with her asshole boyfriend."

"What about the family? The Blandels? Fourth floor?"

"Left last week."

"Et merde."

"Oh, God. I can't do this," I moan under my breath. "Not again."

"Again?"

Ignoring his question, I scrabble around on the elevator wall. Maybe there's an escape hatch or something. A hole I can crawl through or a little cubby with a phone inside. I've seen those before. "There's gotta be a way to call out. You know, a little door somewhere."

"Oh. That's not a bad idea."

"That another shocker for you?"

"What?" His light scans one elevator wall. "Why?"

Now it's my turn to snort. "Look, you've clearly got a thing against women. You've been a jerk to me from day one."

The light swivels and slides up my body to shine right in my eyes. "I like women very much, thank you."

"Please get that out of my face."

It shifts to scan the opposite wall. "*You* were the rude one, actually, the day we met."

"You were staring at my *ass*!"

"Well, you can't blame me for that. It's a lovely arse. And in that little dress, it was—"

"And you—" His words register and my stomach does a weird up and down thing. "What?"

"You know it is," he says, as if I'm refusing to admit to something that's perfectly obvious.

"Actually, I…" *Is* my ass good? I don't know. Maybe? I've never really thought about it, aside from when I used to lament its size. I don't do that anymore. Does my butt get attention? Yes, it does. But it's not always positive and it's frequently unwelcome. "My butt's fine, I guess."

"You *guess*?" The light's focused on the ceiling now,

though I don't think he's looking up there. He's staring at me. "Your arse is fucking spectacular."

"Oh. I..." I swallow the automatic urge to return the compliment. "Okay, then. Um, thanks? I guess."

"Bollocks," he mutters under his breath. "Look, I'm sorry I've been a right pri—"

Something grinds above us, metal to metal, and the elevator jolts so hard my teeth clack together. In the next instant, the world goes pitch black.

CHAPTER SIX

*C*olin

The moment the lift lurches, I reach into the dark and grab her. It's not a conscious decision, but rather instinct shouting at me to keep her safe.

Even after the fucking death trap grinds to a halt, I can't let her go.

I'm pure adrenaline, arms tight, muscles frozen in place. She's tiny, bloody minuscule, and I'm probably smothering her like this, but the shock is fizzing through me and my brain's shorted out and all I can do is hold her.

"Sorry," I finally manage, though for what, I can't be sure.

Her only reply is an audible exhale—shaky, but good enough as far of proof of life goes.

"Christ." I start to pull away.

"Wait. Wait, wait." Her fingers claw at my back, keeping me close.

I stop.

"Don't go. Please. I'm not…"

Nodding, I ease to the side, pressing myself to one wall while turning my stranglehold into more of an embrace, arms winding around her soft back. She clamps onto me like a barnacle.

"You all right?" It's hard to catch my breath.

She nods, tickling my nose with that wad of hair.

"You sure?"

"Yes. Fine. *Great.*"

Slowly, I exhale and take stock. It's full dark now, with my mobile lost somewhere on the floor. I can't imagine we'll get much more from it anyway. Just before the big lurch, the battery was at one percent.

"What, um, what happened?"

"I've no idea. The lift's a right mess."

"Probably haunted, right?"

I shake my head. "If you believe in that nonsense."

"You don't?"

I shift and she follows, fear coming off her in waves. I'm ashamed to admit that I rather enjoy feeling the hero for once, instead of the bastard.

"Not really." I sigh, preparing to destroy any good will between us. "Ghosts are like religion. Crutches invented by people who need something to believe in when life gets rough."

"Whoa." Finally, she eases slightly away. Not entirely, but enough to get a little breathing room. She's still soft, still warm, still close. "Those are some fighting words to be pulling out on Christmas Eve, big guy."

"Yes, well, to me it's a day like any other."

"Of course it is." She edges farther, taking her heat with her. And her goodwill.

I bend, surprised to find the whisky bottle intact at my feet, and locate the mobile. When I touch the screen, nothing happens. I push a side button. No change. Should I tell her that we've lost our light source? I don't really want to. My breathing's leveled out, but hers is still audible, quick and frantic. She's scared.

Wait. What if she's afraid of *me*?

Like a rugby ball to the stomach, our earlier conversation comes back to me and I hang my head in shame, realizing just how inappropriate I've been.

Her arse? Her smell? Christ, what am I doing?

Damn it, Llewelyn, what is wrong with you? It takes a right prick to bring up a woman's body—no matter how fine it is—in a situation like this one. Here we are caught in a stressful, possibly life-threatening mess, and I'm the prat who had to go and talk about the woman's arse, before literally groping her in the dark.

"I must apologize. I shouldn't have said what I did earlier. About your…" Oh, shut it, you twat. "It was inappropriate. And I'm sorry."

"About my butt?" She huffs out a sound that could be a laugh or simply irritation. "It's fine. I…" Another huff. "I appreciate the compliment."

"Yes, well. My timing could use a little work."

"No kidding."

"Truly, though. I mean, yes, you're magnificent, but…" *Abort, mate. You're making a mess of it.* "I don't want you to feel uncomfortable, given the ah, close quarters, all right? Well, feel however you like, obvi-

47

ously. Far be it from me to tell you how to..." *Shut your fucking mouth. Shut it now.* "Listen, why don't you..."

"What?" Is she laughing? I think she's laughing.

"You should say something inappropriate. To, I don't know, balance the scales, if you wish. Or, crap, maybe grope me."

"Grope you?"

"Like I just did you, for which I apolo—"

"Was that groping? I thought you were protecting me?"

"I was."

"Well then, I'm not..." A few seconds pass in silence. "God, how long are we gonna be here?"

I don't bother answering. No point, is there?

"You know what? Sure. I'll balance the scales."

I laugh, surprising myself.

"You want a compliment?"

I'm the one now who's breathing fast. "Whatever you like. Compliment, insult, full-on rant. Pick your poison. I deserve it."

Her dark hum heats the air between us, turning pure fear into something more pleasant. "I already told you what I call you."

"You did. And it *really* hurt."

Her giggle feels like an accomplishment. "I don't believe you."

"All right. The names were too cute to do any real harm."

"Cute? They're mean."

I scoff. "Mean would involve curse words."

"Oh, I don't cuss," she says, as prim and proper as can be. "Well, only in…"

"In what? When you're driving? When your shitty downstairs neighbor storms up after three hours of sleep to tell you to stop cackling like a hyena."

"A hyena? No way."

"All right, like a chicken, then."

The laugh that bursts from her is high and lively and bright and, beyond all comprehension, hits me right in the balls. Maybe it's the fear of death hanging over us. The adrenaline. That after-battle thing that makes people jump into bed together.

Christ, where did that come from? After battle? Is that what this is? The idea thrums through me, settling warm in my bollocks.

"Okay, I'll admit to a slight clucking sound in the higher notes." A pause, full of awareness. "So, do you not laugh, then, McGrumpypants? Like, ever?"

"You don't know my name, do you?"

"It's Llewelyn."

"That's my family name."

"Chucky."

"Like the horror doll? No! What makes you…? Oh, the C on my letterbox."

"Christos?"

"No."

"Uh, Claudius! Clyde? Clementine!"

I'm smiling. "No, no. And clearly not."

"Chortbert?"

"That's not a name."

"Caesar? Carlito?"

My smile turns to a full on grin. "Do you want to know or is guessing fun for you?"

"A little of both. The distraction's helping."

Good. "Are you cold?"

"Yes." Her voice is thin, all humor gone in an instant. "And scared."

"Here. Take my coat." Careful not to bump into her, I work the jacket off, my movements awkward in the small space.

"No. No, I'm fine."

"Bollocks. It's freezing in here. Come on." I reach out, encounter a shoulder, and drape it over her.

"You'll be cold."

"I've got on layers." Not to mention the rush of blood heating my veins. "I'm fine."

At the sound of her shuddering, I reach for the coat —which it feels like she's swimming in—draw the sides together, and bending, zip it up from the bottom, taking care to avoid any contact with her body. "There." I step back, dizzy from the sweet scent of her. "Better." I pat her arms, which is something my father used to do instead of hugging us boys goodbye.

"Thank you," she manages, through teeth that are audibly chattering. "Who…would've guessed…that Clifford "Ebenezer" Llewelyn had a heart after all?"

For fuck's sake. "Why didn't you say you were cold earlier?"

"I…I didn't realize. I think it's shock or something. Also, I had wine tonight and… Wait. Did I leave the oven on? I was going to bake a cake." She moans. "Is it on? I can't remember. Okay. Wait. Wait, so, I went to the kitchen and opened the fridge to take out the butter, got attacked by the killer stink cheese, and..."

"And? What do you reckon? We going to burn to a crisp in this towering inferno?"

"Is it a tower if it's only six floors?"

I smile. "Probably not."

"Okay. I didn't turn it on. I don't think. I'm almost positive."

"All right. Well, that's excellent news." As I relax back, my foot hits the bottle. "And I have more good news."

"Really?"

"Don't get too excited. It's not a way out or anything." With difficulty, I drop into a squat, careful not to rub her inappropriately, grab the whisky from its bag, and hold it up. The most she'll be able to see, even now that our eyes have adjusted, is a glint of light filtering down from the filthy skylight onto glass. "I do, however, have sustenance."

"Food?"

"Booze." I open the bottle and immediately get a nose full of the single malt's burnt peat aroma.

The sound of her inhaling through her nose is bizarrely sensuous. "Smells good."

"Care for a tipple?"

With a long, beaten-sounding sigh, she gives in. "Might as well."

I hold it out and, after a moment, startle at the cold press of her fingers to mine. "Shit, woman, you're a bloody icicle."

"This'll warm me up."

51

I listen as she tips the bottle back and takes what's got to be the world's tiniest sip. Then another. And another.

"Thanks."

I'm probably imagining the few extra seconds she lets her frigid hand linger under my warm one when she returns the bottle. When I slug back a good dose of the stuff, it tastes wildly different from the glass I drank earlier in the pub. It's headier, smokier, more potent.

I hand the bottle back and she accepts it briskly, to my great disappointment.

"So," she starts, her weight making the wall beside me creak. In the dark, every movement comes with its own set of subtle clues to decipher. I wait breathlessly for whatever she'll do next. "You got big plans for tonight?"

"Just this." Her laugh makes me immeasurably pleased. "You?"

"Oh, yeah. Right. Same. Absolutely. Slugging back booze in the elevator with my hated neighbor."

Now, why on earth does that hurt? I'm an idiot. To let it bother me, to give a shit what she thinks, when I've been nothing but a prick to her.

I make a sound that could pass as a laugh. "Right. Well, at least it's good booze. I reckon that'll make up for the company."

She sniggers and sways toward me with the bottle, giving me a little of her weight in the exchange. Her shoulder against my arm. Edging into the crook of my elbow. I like the feel of it there. Just a shoulder and an elbow. Nothing special. Hell, in the metro, I'd hardly notice, but in here, with nothing to look at? It's intense.

I notice things, too. Just how bloody tiny she is in such close quarters. Thick and short. Plump. Which is so fucking appealing, I can't help but give her some weight in return. It's not like I'll get another chance to feel this body against mine. May as well enjoy what she's willing to give.

"It's Colin," I tell her, finally, in a whisper so low she'd never hear me in the real world. But here? Where it's so dark and quiet, alone has a fresh meaning, I reckon she could read my lips from the noise alone. "Colin T. Llewelyn. At your service, Madame."

"Huh. Okay. How d'you do, kind sir?" Her voice goes high and fluty and, this time when I reach out, I get her hand instead of the whisky. It's still cold. Mine engulfs it, tightens slightly. Holds it, suspended. Waiting. Neither of us moves to separate.

"I'm not gonna ask what the T stands for."

"Best not to." I give that little hand a light squeeze. And still, I don't pull away. That's the thing about the dark. You can pretend not to see things, pretend you don't feel them, like they're not happening at all. "Wouldn't want to know too much about the enemy."

"Right. Might humanize him." She squeezes back. Lingers. Pretending, like me. "Lord knows I don't want to do that. The last thing a man like Colin Theophile Llewelyn needs is a bigger head than he already has."

"A big head?" I let my thumb drag over the back of her hand—just a centimeter or two. Not something she'd notice. "Me?"

"Oh, come on. You're hot, you've got the...ridiculously sexy accent, a thriving pub in the center of Paris. I've seen how packed it gets." She has? When? "Don't tell me you're not rolling in admirers."

"Positively smothered by them." I lean in. "But you'll be pleased to know that none of them is as annoying as you."

"Flatterer."

"It's part of my charm." I snort. "Actually, the sum total."

We breathe, holding hands without moving. Waiting, listening, literally suspended in place, in time. Chilly fingers, shuddering breaths, whispered words we'd never have been able to hear through the ceiling of my flat.

"Shall I warm the other, as well?" I ask, hoping like hell she'll give in and say yes.

CHAPTER SEVEN

*J*ules

Warm the other? Yes. Yes, I want that.

Lightheaded and breathless, I turn so we're facing each other, lean my shoulder against the wall for balance, and hold my hand out, whisky bottle and all.

He wraps his hand around mine on the bottle neck and leaves it there so we're gripping it together. A joint effort.

I have to break the silence. "What do you think's gonna happen? To us?"

I feel more than see his upper body cant toward me. "Do you mean will Madame Christen's yapping dog finally wake her up for its three a.m. piss and get us help?"

"Or did she go away for Christmas, too?" The idea scares the crap out of me.

He makes this low, grunty sound, which I think for him might be close to a laugh, and shuttles slightly closer. "That woman hasn't a friend in the world. She's evil. Her furry little devil's spawn's no better. Have you ever *not* been attacked by that creature?"

I picture the woman's little dog, barking its head off in the lobby, while she looks on benignly, and can't help but laugh. Our hands drop, breaking our mutual hold on the bottle, which he's now left with. I ignore how cold I am. "What if you've got it all wrong? What if the dog's barking in a wild bid to get free from the woman's clutches?"

"Oh, that's good. Very good. An SOS. Like it's been kidnapped."

"Yeah. Yeah, and here we are, clueless passersby, while the dog's screaming, like *screaming* at us to help him escape."

"Free me, fucking humans! Get me out of here!"

"God." I accept the bottle from him, back to the wall, and then slide slowly down to land on my butt, knees bent. "Poor thing. How... There's no way of knowing, is there? What if he's just trying and trying, yapping in this wild frenzy, and we're ignoring it."

"Oh, I don't ignore the little fucker."

I stare up at where he's still standing, somehow closer now that I'm down here and my face is near his leg. "You secretly kick it, don't you, you angry man?"

"I'm not angry."

"No? Name one thing you like that isn't grim."

"Grim? I like things that aren't grim."

"No. You like things that are grim. And ghoulish, violent. Sometimes gross." Sometimes sad.

"What are you—"

"*The Thing? Scarface?*"

"I like happy things."

I make a disbelieving noise. "Name one Christmas movie you've watched."

It's his turn to snuffle cynically. "I've not watched any."

"None? At all?"

"Not that I remember." He hums. "Oh, wait. *Die Hard*. That's a—"

"Absolutely not." I'm shaking my head and smiling, despite myself. "No way. That's an action movie that happens to take place on Christmas. Not the same."

"All right. Name a classic. Something I should see before I die."

"Uh, *Miracle on 34th Street. It's a Wonderful Life! A Christmas Carol.*"

"That's a book."

"Yeah, well, there are like a million movie versions. Even the Muppets did one, so—"

"I've watched *Nightmare Before Christmas.*"

I roll my eyes so hard he can probably see the whites in the dark. "Oh wait, hold on! I know. You're from the UK. How about *Love, Actually?*"

"Oh, for fuck's sake." His voice echoes through the tiny space, loud down here, as if his head's tilted my way. "No!"

"What? Are you kidding? Why not?"

"Don't tell me you think it's romantic."

"It *is*!"

"Bollocks! It's crap! It's absolute shite. A bunch of stories, or whatever, about good people getting shafted or settling or, God, you should know this, it's all about women being given the short end of the stick. Over and over and over again. What is it about that stupid film that makes people think it's better than it is? Not a Christmas movie, by the way. Not even a little."

"Well, I beg to differ. I mean, I guess I see that Emma Thompson storyline's not the most feminist, but there's the Hugh Grant one, right? It's sweet and, oh, oh, the Colin Firth story with the Portuguese woman, who—"

"You mean the cleaner? His *employee*, who literally can't understand a word the rich, foreign visitor's saying? That's romantic, is it? Abuse of power? And Hugh Grant's the bloody prime minister, right? Most powerful person in Great Britain. Honestly. It's fucking shocking that... Oh, and the worst one. The bloody worst of them all is the Keira Knightley subplot, which is morally, ethically *fucked*." He's not wrong, I concede. I've always felt weird about that one. "Do you know how old she was when she played that role? Barely legal is how old. The bloke's a lying, cheating bastard and she's—"

"It's sweet and sad! Unrequited love. The poor man feels he has to tell her before he can move on! Come on. There are other good stories in the movie, about people who are well-meaning and kind and do the right thing."

"Right. Like Laura Linney caretaking her brother and missing out on the hottest night of her life with a man that most women I know would sell their left tit to snog, given the chance. That's your *right* thing, is it?" I can hear the air quotes in that sentence. "Could you tell me how that can possibly be construed as romantic? It's bloody not. No. No, it's certainly not a Christmas film. And if it is…" The sigh he lets out is heavy, almost beaten, despite him pretty much making his point. "If that's what it's all about, I'd rather not celebrate." After a pause, he says, "Sorry. My world view's crap sometimes."

Another pause. Ticking somewhere close by, like pipes heating or going cold. His breathing's loud, like the grit under his soles as his feet shuffle beside me.

"I hate Christmas anyway, so bah humbug." Fabric ghosts against the side of my face.

Instead of chasing it with my cheek, I dig deeper into the coat. It's warm and soft on the inside. The lining's slick. Silk, maybe. It feels expensive. Heavy. Substantial. "I don't hate it."

I remember the pine needle scent of the tree when Dad would drag it inside, fresh from the Boy Scouts' lot. It was always too tall and he'd have to use a worn, wide-toothed saw to take off the stump and get sawdust on the floor. It was a mess to clean up, but it didn't feel like work with Louis Armstrong singing that he had his love to keep him warm. "Christmas is the best."

At least it used to be.

"Yeah? What about it?"

"Togetherness. Giving." Sharing music and laughs and food that smelled rich and warmed my insides. Too many sweets for my teeth and my stomach, but just the right amount for my soul. "Being a part of something."

He snorts. "And for the poor, infirm, and alone?"

"I'm alone tonight. I'm fine." I almost mean it, too. "Come on. You've got to see some good in it."

"No. I don't."

I nudge his leg with my shoulder. "Maybe you'll change your mind." I want him to. I wish this for him.

"I doubt it." A pause. "There room down there for another?"

I consider. What is he asking, really? Is there subtext here? Do I *want* there to be?

Yes. I do.

I want to—I swallow, the sound loud in the suspended silence, and let my head thunk back against the metal side—kiss him. I know that in here, his lips will feel like so much more than they would out there in the world, the light, the sounds and sights, the way his hand did. The way his voice is so close, it's almost inside my head. The way I can smell woodsmoke on him, detergent through cold denim, without even touching.

It's a *terrible* idea. I mean, the man doesn't even like Christmas, for crying out loud.

But he held me when he thought the elevator was falling. He gave me his coat. He thinks my ass is stupendous and that I'm magnificent and I'm leaving Paris soon, so...

"Yeah." I scoot toward the front of the elevator and wait with bated breath to see which way he'll choose to sit. Not that it'll mean anything. Or maybe it will?

When he slides down close beside me, putting our shoulders together at one end and our feet at the wall opposite, I can't decide if it's on purpose or random or if I'm being really, really ridiculous right now.

"Ah, this is better," he says in that low, secret voice I've only heard in the confines of this little metal box. A voice just for me. "Is it warmer down here or am I imagining it?"

"See? You're cold! Oh my God. You should take this back. I'll be—"

"Frozen stiff by morning." He pushes my arm down before I can move to slide the enormous coat off. "Absolutely not."

The hand he held me back with is still on my arm. It's warm, I think, although there's no way I can feel it through the jacket's down filling. My imagination's working overtime, I guess. But then it always has with this man.

Since that first day, I've pictured conversations where I insult him with a cutting cynical wit he can't begin to come back from until he begs me to accept his apologies and brings me to a tiny off-the-beaten-path restaurant that only real Parisians know about, with a cozy handful of tables and a menu written out on a chalkboard, and orders all the desserts because he knows how I feel about chocolate. Then, for a nightcap, we swing by his quiet pub and he lights the little fire in that marble and pressed tin fireplace—just for me—and gives me, well, I guess it'll be a scotch when I picture it now, although it was always cognac before, and then he sits next to me on a bar stool and leans in, smelling like—

"You all right there, love?"

"Huh?" I startle back to reality, a little dizzy, a little shocked, quite frankly, to find myself here, in this place with him and not daydreaming on my own upstairs. "Sorry. Got a little...distracted." Oh, no. No, that's not the word I meant to use, I meant to say tired or drowsy. Now, he'll think it's his presence that's done it to me, which is definitely the truth, but he doesn't need that confirmation.

"Uh, Jules?"

I jump again, my eyes massive as I stare at him, through him, maybe into the dark beyond him. "You know my name."

"Well, yes. Yes, I do."

Heat—or some bloodborne facsimile—fizzles across my face. "How?"

He clears his throat, a little awkwardly, and shifts the tiniest bit away from me. "Must've heard it or seen it on a letter or something."

Hm. Okay. I guess that's possible.

"Your poor legs. They've got to be freezing."

At his words, I shudder. "I'm fine." Except I don't sound fine. And, maybe it's the booze that's made my brain all hazy or maybe it's his presence. Probably it's the cold. I mean, it is freaking bone-chilling in here.

"That's complete bollocks. Listen. Why don't you..." He scooches until our thighs are pressed tightly together, sets a hot hand on my leg and pulls it back fast, as if he's been bitten. "Sorry. God, I shouldn't. You're just so..."

"Sexy, I know." I giggle. And then hiccup to a shocked stop. What am I doing? Why would I go and *say* something like that, when there's nowhere to run? No way to get out of here and hide? Crap, am I drunk? On the whisky or something else?

"Well, you are sexy." I am? Oh god, what is happening? "But you're going to freeze to death like that."

"The floor *is* cold." My shoes drop from my ice cube feet with a thud.

"Shit. It's frigid. Can I... Look, I promise not to do anything. I do. I..." He grunts in apparent frustration, then inhales, slow and deep and so loud I imagine I can feel it. "Look. What if you sat on my lap?"

"Oh, I—"

"Nothing weird from me. I promise. Absolutely."

"I don't want to—"

"Look, I promise on on on my...my brother's grave, all right?"

Between us, silence. Around us, that ticking, a scuffle in a some far off hidey hole. Way, way in the distance a car horn.

My mouth presses tightly shut.

"I mean it. I'm worried you'll get hurt. Permanently. And the whisky feels good, but it's not going to get these legs warmed up. This is dangerous. Truly. It's near zero degrees out there. Come on. No arguing. Up you go." He slides an arm behind my back and gets me onto his lap with no apparent effort.

The surface of his jeans is cold against my skin, but beneath, the man is pumping out heat. I'm immediately ten degrees warmer.

With a sigh, I lean back, let him wrap his arms around me and pull me in tight to his thick chest. God, he's big. I mean, I'm short, so everyone towers over me. And the man's not particularly tall, compared to a lot of guys—Maybe five ten or eleven?—but he's sturdy in a way that I like. Hefty bones and muscles. Just thinking about it reminds me of that dark happy trail I did my very best not to look at this morning and remember every second of my day in the chocolaterie and, yes, I'll admit, in the warmth of the apartment earlier tonight.

I squirm a little thinking of the sheer number of times I've fantasized about this guy and how wrong that suddenly seems, especially given this new safety-driven seating arrangement.

"Here, turn to the side. Curl up." He gets me settled so my cheek is against the very object of my daydreams and I can smell him and up close, he smells *wonderful*. "There." He runs a hand from the top of my hair down my back, then wraps himself around me so I'm cocooned in his arms. It's so warm here, I've got no choice but to nestle in deeper and sigh. "Good? All right?" With my ear to his chest, his voice is a deep, comforting bass. I love this rumbling sound. A sound from my childhood. A sound from when I had every-thing I could possibly want and had no idea I'd one day lose it.

It's probably the booze that brings the prick of tears to my eyes. I don't know. I'm cold and scared and this is not what I thought I'd be doing tonight, but also, I don't hate this moment.

I sniffle and he shifts.

"Jules?"

"Yeah," I whisper, so quiet against him there's a chance he doesn't hear.

"I don't hate you."

I go absolutely still. "I don't hate you either, Colin."

The hand on my shoulder tightens for a second and loosens. His breath warms the top of my head and he says, a smile in his voice, "You don't smell like cheese anymore."

My pulse picks up. And then, entirely unable to stop myself, I ask, "What do I smell like?"

CHAPTER EIGHT

*C*olin

Closing my eyes, I inhale again. There's a lot to parse through, in the background. Odors I'd not usually notice—metal and rubbish, Madame Christen's curried lentils, that flowery cleaning product the concierge uses.

I bury my nose in her hair. "Like spun sugar." I don't mention the hint of soap, the sweat. The human smells no one likes to be reminded of. Smells that turn me on and make me want to dig deeper, taste, lick.

She lets out a low hum that I feel in my abdomen. And lower. "I've been working in a patisserie/choco-laterie."

I shift back just enough to look down at her, though there's not much to see. "Yeah? Which one?"

"Duchesne, around the corner. I just work the register, but they're such good people and the chocolatier's been teaching me some stuff. Have you been there?"

"Yes, as a matter of fact. I was there today. Didn't see

you, though." Arsehole that I am, I'd probably have avoided the place if I'd known she worked there.

"What did you get?"

"Oh, just a bûche de noel. For a friend."

"Really? Well, it is entirely possible that I made those little mushrooms on top. Cécile's been showing me how to make perfect meringues."

"I'm impressed."

"Oh, I just mess around."

"You made meringues that were sold in one of the best patisseries in the city. That's not exactly messing around." I deliver the two last words with a terrible American accent.

"Huh. I hadn't considered that. It's just a job, you know? I got it through a friend. Unofficial and everything. Besides, I'm taking off soon."

My stomach clenches. "Oh? Where to?"

"There's work waiting for me in Milan."

"Ah. Moving up to Master Chocolatier? Or is it Mistress?"

"That sounds naughty." I refrain from responding and let her go on. "No, just helping out in a shop."

"What kind of shop?"

"I don't remember, actually. Clothes? Or maybe a tourist thing? It's not about the job, it's about the experience. I just...traveling's what I do. The rest is..." She makes a hand movement that I can't see. In its wake, the air moves. Nothing but a shift of particles that I feel against the back of my hand.

"Sounds rather exciting." Her silence speaks volumes

and when I go on, my voice is gentler, the words almost a question. "Or not?"

"Yeah, no, it *is* exciting."

"All right." I settle back, enjoying her weight and, if I'm being honest, the conversation, too. She's interesting, bright, easy to chat with.

"Crap."

"What?" I loosen my hold. "You all right?"

"I don't want to go." From her voice, I'd say this is a realization she's just now having.

"Then don't."

"It's not that easy."

I say nothing.

"I like it here."

"In Paris?" *Or in my arms?*

"Yeah. The shop. This building. Friends... Neighbors."

"Except the git on the 5th floor. That bastard can get right off."

The light thump of her hand smacking my shoulder puts a smile on my face. I wonder if she's smiling, too, and for a moment, I consider reaching out to touch her lips in order to find out.

"That obnoxious British guy? Jury's still out on him."

"What?" I don't consider what I'm doing before poking a finger in her ribs. Can't quite reach her through the thick coat, but still she squirms and giggles. Within seconds, we're tussling on the elevator floor. She's laughing, I'm grinning like a fool. I *wish* I could see her face. Is she flushed? Are those wide blue eyes hazy and unfocused? And her mouth. God, her mouth. What's it doing?

Shit, I want her. And not just that, which is bad enough. I actually *like* her. A lot.

I've got to get out of here. I can't fall for this American with her round, pink face and her sweet scent and that biting edge of humor that I'd never in a million years have guessed was hiding behind the sugary sweet facade. I can't...

She moves again, gathering her limbs up tighter into a knot on my lap and, in the process, rubbing that heavy arse against my cock. That bastard apparently doesn't give a shit about my promise to keep this from getting weird. With every shift, every hint of friction, it's warming and thickening and if she doesn't quit that—

Her next twist of limbs moves her so she's straddling me and, in the blink of an eye, the air changes.

Everything changes. Our breathing, the sounds around us, Christ, I think the dark's gotten darker.

"Stop that." My hands tighten, holding her in place.

She doesn't respond. Doesn't budge. Doesn't breathe, I don't think.

For a handful of seconds, we sit completely frozen, both probably listening to the other trying not to make a sound. Both waiting.

Only one of us wanting, though.

"Are you...all right?" She finally breaks the silence, her voice low and breathy.

My "Fine" is a strained, transparent lie.

"I'm too heavy, right?" She moves as if to rise. "Sorry. I should have—"

"No. No, not at all."

I let her struggle to standing. I can't exactly keep her on my lap against her will, can I?

"Sure," she replies, her voice thick.

Shit. Shit, shit.

"Jules, I..." I huff out an impatient breath. "You weren't too heavy. You're not heavy. You're..." *Perfect. I know your weight now, know how every gram feels in my arms, on my thighs. I know how your skin sounds against denim. I know how you smell up close.*

"Listen. Seriously, it's fine. I'm used to it. Just part of being a plus size—"

"No!" I exclaim a little too loudly, offended. "I was having an unfortunate reaction."

"Reaction?"

I clear my throat and thunk my head back against the wall once. Twice. It knocks hollowly, its volume more painful than the contact. Finally, my voice a dry, ragged, raspy thing, I say, "To your stupendous arse." Amongst other things.

Her inhalation is audible. "Oh."

"Sorry."

"Well, that's fine. It's a perfectly natural—"

"Could we find a new topic of conversation? Please?"

"Oh, sure. Yeah. Ummmmm..."

I wrack my brain for something—anything—to draw attention from my now-aching cock and come up with, "So, you worked today, then?"

"Yep. Yes. Definitely." The floor creaks. I imagine it's her shifting her weight from one foot to the other and back. The dark is uncomfortable now, as full as it was a moment ago, only now it's awkward and wrong. "I go in early. Five, usually. Six today, because I stayed late last night, doing the meringues. And, you know, with Italy coming up, there wasn't time to see my grandmother for the holidays, so I just...stayed."

"Is that all right? Not too lonely?"

She marches lightly in place. To keep warm, I'm guessing. I picture those little feet, her plump, painted toes getting blue from the cold. I think of warming her legs again, pressing those toes between my knees, my hands. My cock jerks. I reach down and press hard on it, wishing it would go down. But the prick's got a thing for this woman. Can't say I blame the poor bastard.

"What about you? Did you work tonight?"

"Yeah. It was crap."

"Busy?"

"Slow. People are gone. Or with family. No one's going to the pub tonight. Just a couple of the usual punters."

"What about you? No family?" She sounds tentative.

"My parents are back in Wales. I can't..." Can't *stand* going there. The silence, the still, stale smell of loss.

I reach for the bottle, relieved when my knuckles knock on body-warmed glass, and unscrew the top to slug back a mouthful before the memories come crowding in. There's no way to fight them here in the dark.

"I'm sorry, Colin."

I swipe my sleeve over my mouth. "What for?"

"You said something about your brother's grave earlier and I should have let it go. Why didn't I? I knew it was a touchy subject and went and asked about your family anyway. I do that sometimes. I'm so sorry. Why do I always have to push and push—"

"You didn't push. What are you—"

"That's my MO." More shifting, her body dancing as far from mine as it can, her antsy moves playing the insides of our little tin bucket like a timpani. "You know. Here's a tough nut, better crack it. I mean, you're this grumpy, bitter—"

"Bitter?"

"Brooding guy—"

"Slight improvement."

"And every time I see you, I just want to, like, ruffle you up and get into your brain or something. Maybe even get you to smile and figure out why you're so frowny and grunty."

"I don't think those are words."

"But I get it. I get that men often hold things inside— and society tells you that's how to be, so it's understand- able—and you're such a stoic guy with your... massive...big..."

"Big what?" It's a shock to find that I'm grinning.

"Ah, hell," she breathes. "Can I please have the bottle?"

"With pleasure." I hand it over, bumping up against her gooseflesh-covered thigh. She grabs it from me and when our hands meet this time, there's no doubt that the touch is purposeful. From her, from me. Her fingers twine around mine, tighten, and finally loosen with a slow stroke.

Perhaps we tried to hide it earlier, but this is direct.

Intended. It's affectionate, almost. But that can't possibly be real, can it? Not after all the animosity these past months.

I hear the series of bird sips she takes and wonder when we'll have to stop using the bottle for drinking and start using it as a receptacle for something else.

She takes another tipple. I consider telling her to slow down and then decide that I'm in no position to be policing the woman. Especially not when she hands the whisky back. I go to take more and stop.

Though my earlier plan was to get right pissed, it's no longer what I want. Not here. Not with her. I set the whisky to the side and sit back.

"I talk too much sometimes. Sorry, Colin."

"No need."

"Seriously. Nana calls it the Wall o' Words. It's like a tidal wave when it hits. Blaaaaaaaaaaaahhhh."

"Stop apologizing," I tell her, allowing myself the quickest touch of her foot. "I don't mind."

I don't just hear the exhaustion in her long, drawn-out sigh, I feel it. I suppose that's what happens when the dark crushes in.

"I was in this car crash." I don't say a word when she starts talking. "I was seven. They, uh…" She swallows. Who knew that could be such an emotional sound? I fight the urge to stand and take her in my arms, forcing myself instead to stay completely still, folded up on the floor, back to the wall. "Dad was driving and my mom died."

"Shit, Jules." I push up to standing. "I'm—"

She steps back. "It's okay."

"The *fuck* it is." The urge to reach out is strong.

"I just mean I'm used to it. It's my story now. It's who I am."

"Right." I know the feeling. The pure resignation of having lived through something. Having lost someone. I force my body back, give her space.

"I got trapped in the car." The way she's giving me the story, without much inflection, even-toned, like she's told it over and over again, makes me want to protect that little girl with my life. Seven fucking years old. "The emergency people—they were amazing. Just great. It took them ages to get me out. You know, those big jaws of life and everything. There was this one woman—a firefighter. Bianca. She sang songs with me the whole time they worked. I was stuck upside down and she spent, you know, *forever* on the other side of the car just telling stories and singing. And asking me to sing." I hear the shrug in her voice, minimizing the experience. Making it palatable. Something she can fold up and store deep inside her. She's grown up without a mother, for fuck's sake, and she's boiled it down to a casual story.

My heart—a shriveled, bloodless thing—twists upon itself like a dry sponge. The pain's unbearable.

"You must have been terrified."

My words feel solid in the space between us. Each one a pointless ping against her cold skin.

"I wasn't alone, you know? Bianca was there."

"What about your dad?"

"What about him?"

"Where was he throughout this?"

The hard huff of air she lets out tells me that it's not her favorite subject and I let it lie.

Her sniffle—quiet though it is—makes me move toward her in a flash. I don't need my eyes to know where her body is. Our shapes are black holes and hers draws me straight in. I wrap her in my arms and she responds by clamping herself around my middle, face pressed into my chest, giving me the fiercest hug of my life. I give it back. Take it, return it. Touching, holding. It's so much more just now. Is it the stillness? Is it that hanging above the world like this, we've developed a new gravitational pull? Not towards Earth, but each other.

I can't let her go just now.

"Thank you," she whispers.

"There's nothing to thank me for, love."

"There is. You're here." It comes out muffled against my shirt. "I'm not alone."

I tighten my arms and hold on to her for dear life. With a lurch that's almost sickening, I fall, hard and fast.

It's almost a shock, when I take stock, that the lift is still suspended, still dark and quiet, aside from the loud thumping of my heart in my chest.

She's given me a gift just now, by opening up, showing me her tender insides, and though I can't begin to explain why, I'm compelled to reciprocate.

"Eddie, my brother, was twenty-six." I let the words spill into the chill air, my arms around her, our connection rock solid. "I was two years older. I worked in the City."

"Here?"

"London. In finance. I was a right bastard." I make an ugly noise. "An entitled little prick with no fucking clue what it meant to live and work and be...human."

"I doubt you were that—"

"Come on, Jules. You've seen how rotten I can be. Trust me when I say that this is me deep in my shiny, happy phase. I was a young white prat who cared about three things: making money, playing rugby, and going down the pub with my mates. Add in frequent, random, heartless shags and that was my ideal life." I pause, giving her a chance to judge me. "Ebenezer Scrooge is spot on, actually. That was me."

Her body shakes with what I think is laughter before she unwinds her arms and shifts back, leaving me cold, bereft. We're each on our own side of the lift now and, although we're less than a step from one another, after all the physical intimacy, it feels as though we're worlds apart.

Good. At least she won't have to shove me away when I tell her. I suddenly can't bear the idea of feeling her horror against me.

Bracing myself, I drop my truth bomb with all the delicacy of the City trader I am at heart. "So, when I tell you that my brother died and it was entirely my fault. You have got to believe me."

CHAPTER NINE

*J*ules

Forget roller coasters. Get stuck in a Paris elevator with the hottest, grumpiest man you've ever met and let the feelings fly. Now, this is what I call a ride. Ups and downs like you wouldn't believe.

I can hardly catch my breath, can't move at all as I wait for him to go on, staying as quiet as I can possibly be. How else can I gauge what's behind the words? I can't see his face, but in this short time, I've somehow learned to...feel his expression, to sense it or hear it. Carefully, I pull his jacket tighter, ignoring how the wood smoke/man smell keeps tricking me into feeling safe.

"He—Eddie—was a pipeline welder. He traveled all over the world working with different crews. From one day to the next, he'd get sent out, stay someplace new, someplace wild and different for him. Brazil, France, Australia. Always traveling. I reckon you'd have got on with him." There's a smile in his voice when he says, "He'd have liked you. I know that."

I hum a wordless reply and stare at where his dark shape curves in on itself.

"His dream was this thing we'd always talked about, he and I. Owning a little pub in Paris. I remember the exact moment we dreamt it up, too." His words tumble out, fast and low, like they've just been waiting to escape. His breathing's gone all quick and choppy. "Mum's French. She always wanted to come back, but Dad is as Welsh as a person can get. Every year, as children, we came here on holiday, to visit Mum's family and sightsee and, for Dad, to get a taste of the expat life. We'd go to a little Scottish pub not far from here. God, Dad was in Heaven. Mum loved it, too, actually. We'd be out all day and, in the evenings, swing by for a tipple before dinner and it felt like, I don't know, a taste of home." He huffs out a breath. "It sounds so infantile now. And so fucking *colonial* to need a pub when there are dozens of cafés. Anyway. Sorry. I'm going on a bit."

He's not going on at all. He's telling his story with the kind of deadpan delivery that I gave just a few minutes ago. Quick, too, like if he doesn't rush, he'll never get it out. Or he'll lose the courage.

Being here in the dark made it easier to let go of my hot, festering wounds. Does he feel the same or is every word as painful as it sounds scraping over his throat?

"I'm listening," I urge. Is it selfish that I want his story? Not to collect it, but to protect it, tight inside this coat. Can he feel that I'm here? There? With him in his pain the way he was with me when I shared mine. Stuck

WE'LL NEVER HAVE PARIS

beside me, inside the car, hanging upside down, singing songs I didn't know. Songs I've tried hard not to think of again.

Because I don't believe for a second he hurt his brother. Not this big, tender man whose heart is so fragile he has to hide it beneath so many layers.

"Right. Eddie always... *We* talked about opening a pub here and I liked the idea, but then I moved on and made, fuck, just so much cash and Eddie went off and did his thing. He'd bring up the pub. I'd nod and say *alri'* and then one day, after years of working the pipeline, he told me he was ready to do it. Had the cash and everything and I..."

He swipes his hand through his hair. The sound quick and rough, like he's trying to hurt himself. A little self-flagellation. A pained exhale. I want to comfort him, the way he did me, but that's not what he's asking for. If I had to guess, I'd say he's seeking punishment.

"I told him I'd changed my mind, you see? I chose playing rugger with my mates, pretentious bars, and my huge flat with views of the Thames over my own fucking *brother*." The low sound he lets out might have started as bitter humor, but once it hits the air, it's something else, charred and angry and stunted. His breath's coming fast, like he's running a race. His body's swaying just the slightest bit. With a big sniff, he gathers himself and straightens. Even in the dark, I can feel the way he's standing at attention, ready to take a hit. Geared up for whatever retribution he seems to think he deserves.

"Now you see, *Jules*," he sneers, trying to put distance

between us, but only reminding me that we're both *right here.* "Instead of safely pouring pints in a Paris pub with his selfish prick of a big brother, Eddie died on the job two months later. Christmas Eve, to be exact. A pipeline explosion. I'll spare you the details."

"Oh no." Sadness bursts through me. "Colin."

He faces the corner, like he's willing himself out. Away. *"Don't."* That one broken word's the loneliest sound I've heard in my life.

"I'm so sorry."

"Don't feel sorry. Feel enraged. Get...angry. Hate me, if you want. Hate works. It burns, cauterizes, gets rid of everything else." He turns to me and back. Turns and back, the still air swishing madly with each shift. I think he'd start pacing if the space allowed. *"Fuck.* If you could see my parents. They're zombies. Hollow, pale, wafer-thin shells, walking, talking, but not alive. Certainly not living."

"What about you?" I ask, out of breath like I've run up six flights. "Are you alive? Are you living?" Or does he hate himself too much to do that?

"I'm here, aren't I? It's enough, isn't it?" He's gotten louder now, not yelling, but blasting like a furnace. Spewing air and heat and regret so it fills the elevator like lava. I can picture his face. Tense, tight, fiercely angry.

"I bought the pub and the flat and I...I open every day. Every. Night. I'm here. *There.* Doing what he wanted. Living his dream for him."

I don't dare touch him now.

"Why? Why did he dream of that? What was it he wanted?"

"I don't fucking know, do I? Maybe he just wanted to drink on the job?" The laugh he lets out is dry as old newsprint. I picture his parents in their house, the way he described them. Hollow, pale, wafer-thin shells.

He's the opposite of that. He's hot enough to set the night on fire. I feel his solid mass, his energy, despite the way he's tried to tamp himself down. It's that anger, maybe. The way it leaks out, even now, in hot, hard puffs.

After a handful of seconds, his breathing slows, the fire banks. I want to put my hand on his chest, to soak up a dose of all that guilt.

Finally, he sighs and goes on, voice lower, tired. "All that traveling. He thought it would be a piece of home, I suppose. A bit of familiarity in a world full of strangers."

Each word pierces me. Tiny, razor sharp.

"I get that." Or something like it. To me, home is a bittersweet ideal that I can't begin to believe in. Not for myself, at least, although I see how others might want it. After the accident, Dad made a brand new life for himself. A house, a family. His home, but never mine. I spent as much time as I could at Nana's. I guess she's home to me, in some ways. "What about you?" The floor creaks as I ease closer. "What's *your* dream?"

"Dream?"

"Your brother had the pub. What did you have?"

"Don't know, to be honest." A weird sound comes from him. Not a sigh, but a rough huff of air, lost in the cold. "No point dreaming, is there?"

81

"But before. You must have imagined something for yourself."

"I don't know. What does anyone want? I was a wanker, living the empty life I *thought* I wanted. Driven by some pathetic need to be more, have more, more, more. I know better now."

"Oh, yeah? What do you know?"

"I know there *isn't* more. This is it."

"God, that's…" Sad, I was going to say, before reconsidering. Is this it? This life. These experiences, these moments? Maybe he's right. Maybe what matters is who we are and what we're given and the rat race is pointless and we should be glad to have ourselves. Not to mention the moments, the time, the opportunities we're given.

Opportunities.

The thought sizzles in the air, against my chilled skin, on my breath.

I take a half step toward him, slowly this time, cautiously. Then my bare foot hits his sneaker and I stub my toe and let out a loud "Ow, crap!" and sort of fall onto him and he catches me and pulls me in and, this time, it's him doing the hugging. Him with his arms holding me to him with his face pressed to the top of my head.

"Colin."

He grunts.

"Tonight? This? What's happening. It's so…" *Miraculous.*

I can't quite work up the courage to say it.

"Fucked?"

"No. *No!* I mean, getting stuck, yes, but being here. With you, after the animosity between us. It's *real*. Can't you feel it? You and me, stuck like this, tonight of all nights. It's… Wait. Don't laugh."

"I won't. Promise." The R is a little rolled, like maybe his Welsh accent's coming through more than before.

I don't mention that he already broke one promise tonight when he got a stiffy earlier because, if I did, I'd be compelled to admit how wet I'd been and how the friction between our bodies did things to my insides and that felt so freaking good that I didn't mind his erection at all. Hell, I wanted it. I still want it, along with the rest of him. The body and the person inside it. When did that happen?

"This feels fated, Colin," I force myself to tell him. "Fated and surprising, real and somehow *important*, you know?"

He shakes his head. His arms loosen, but I don't want that. I want to stay like this, cocooned in his warmth, sharing this thing we've broken open and left bruised and bleeding between us. When he drops his arms, I tighten my hold. "Don't."

"Don't what?" he rasps out, voice unrecognizable.

"Don't let me go. Don't leave." Even as I say the words, I recognize their irony. I'm the one who leaves. Me. Every time.

"Listen, I can't… I promised I wouldn't… What is happening here? What are we doing? We're not meant to be here. There's no such thing as bloody fate. This isn't fate, it's attraction. And if we… When you…" He lets out a pained grunt. "You're so fucking *irresistible*, Jules."

"So don't resist."

His "*Fuck*" is a harsh exhale.

"Kiss me," I whisper, sounding shaky and desperate and only half as hungry for his touch as I am.

Before my next breath, I'm spun, my back slammed to the wall. The cold surface hardly registers.

"I want—"

"Do it." I egg him on. "Whatever it is, do it."

With a growl, he's on me.

CHAPTER TEN

*C*olin
     The dark pares everything down to bursts of sensation. Takes away the trappings of civilization. Leaves me wild. Out of control and more animalistic than I've ever let myself be.

My hands fist her soft hair, calluses snag as I twist and pull close. Rough cheek to smooth. Our noses bump, hard enough to bring tears to my eyes, but even the tears are right.

I want to make it last, to feel every moment of this kiss, this first connection, but I can't. I need this. Her. Like air, like light.

"Come here," I mutter, tightening my fingers in her long curls, gratified by the answering twist of her hands in my shirt, dragging me closer while I fight to do the same. And it's not fast enough. Not deep enough when our lips meet, not hot enough from our tongues twirling, not wet enough, not...enough. Not nearly. Not even fucking close.

She's an experience. Kissing her isn't the sickly sweet thing I'd imagined. It's not stuffing my face with spun sugar, it's a deep, luxurious dive that is so right, it's almost familiar.

This one, my brain chants as I change my angle and lick inside her mouth. This. This.

The sounds I'm making don't come from me. Or at least not the part of myself I show the world, not the part I control. In the shadows, something else has taken over—the snarling, feral creature I keep chained deep inside the basement of my soul. Now that it's out, I'm ruined. We both are.

My hands are everywhere, sliding the coat off her shoulders, pulling our bodies tight together and then pushing, pushing her hard against the metal wall. Her back connects with a clang and a gasp. She twists closer, grasps my face and holds it still. Our heads tilt, our teeth connect in a movement that should be awkward, but resounds in my bones like the clash of swords on the battlefield. A necessary destruction.

There's nothing to see in the dark. Nothing to hide behind.

Cold lips, hot tongue, her smell close up a warm, sweet secret just for me.

I manage to pull away and catch a breath, barely. "Christ."

"What? Am I too—"

I don't let her finish. I need more. Fuck me, I'll never come down from this. I'd better not. I want the edgy urgency, the heedless disregard for comfort. I bite her lip, she returns the favor with a moan. I tug her hair so hard she whimpers, her hands snaking down my back to slide into my waistband.

In retaliation, I press my hips to hers, the hard bar of my cock a threat and a promise. "Stop bloody squirming," I say. "Or I'll lose it."

I will anyway. Her lips are much too soft, too plush. When she pulls at me with just the right amount of pressure, I thank God there's no light. Actually seeing her on top of all this sensation would be too much.

"What happens then?" She sounds as if she's run one of those bloody fell races where you're as likely to lose an eye as finish the damned thing. "If you lose it?"

I give her pelvis another thrust, but it's not enough, God damn it. I need more. Closer, harder, harsher. Both hands skim down the lush, round body I think of all too often, cup her arse to get her as tight against me as I can, encounter only bare skin, and go still.

"What..." With her soft, naked cheeks in my hands, I can barely breathe, can barely think, aside from this strobe-flashing need to taste, take, have. Nothing moves but our heaving chests. "...the *fuck* are you wearing, little girl?" I ask, the last two words scratched out from that dark place I've unwisely unlocked inside me.

"Shorts," she says, her voice only half there. The rest has been scratched away, the shavings of it left on the floor of this free-hanging metal box, along with every one of my inhibitions.

With the little control I've got left, I slide my hands up, then back down and under her waistband, slow enough to give her time to protest. She doesn't, of

87

course. Judging from the rhythmic pulsing of her hips, she wants this as much as I do.

"Where," I ask, as careful and controlled as I can. "Are your fucking knickers?"

"Is that another word for underwear? How many—"

I let out an impatient growl.

Her response is a whispered rush. "I'm not wearing any."

"You mean to tell me you've been bare arsed under those tiny shorts this whole time?"

Her sigh is a long, drawn out exhalation. "Maybe."

With another uncontrolled noise, I drop to the floor so fast I've got to pin her flank to the wall to keep her from collapsing on top of me. The way the lift shudders should be frightening, but my rational brain's nowhere to be found.

Who gives a fuck when you're about to get a taste of the pussy you've been dreaming of for months?

The pajama bottoms are tiny, loose, stretchy things and, rather than yank them down the way my inner monster would like, I urge her legs open and bury my face in the front.

"My god, your smell." Made for me. I breathe her in like the finest, rarest whisky. Something to be savored with every sense before consuming, one slow sip at a time. But I can't do slow. Not now when she's here, smelling like sweetness and spice and sin combined and it just so happens to be the chemical compound of my dreams. "I've got to taste you, love."

"Yes," she whispers. "Okay. Yes. Yes."

My hand grasps the crotch of her ridiculous

garment, yanks it to the side, and before it's cleared her pussy, I dive in, sinking my whole face into her, coating myself with her, marking myself, consuming. Fuck, fuck me.

I'm lost to that part of me that wants to take and take. The part that's wanted to push her up against the letterboxes and rut since the very moment she walked into the building.

That part knew what it wanted, even if my working brain denied it. That part felt the pull. The hunger.

Even tongue-deep inside her, I'm afraid that inner beast will never get enough.

Worse, though, I'm afraid it doesn't want to be sated. It wants more. More of this heavenly taste, more of her almost pained whimpers filling the lift. More of the hunger itself.

I swipe up, flick her stiff little clit with the tip of my tongue, and allow myself a slow, side to side journey back down. "More," I groan, tugging at her lip with my teeth, twisting my head to the side to lick inside her. She's thrown one of her thick thighs over my shoulder and I want every bit of her on top of me, I want to soak up her weight, smother in all this hot, tender flesh.

Above me, her whimper turns to a squeal as I yank the shorts down and tug at her legs.

"What are you doing?" She smacks my hand. "Stop it."

I freeze. "Shit. You all right?"

"We're in an elevator."

"I need to get my face in your gorgeous pussy, Jules. Please."

"You do?"

"So badly."

"Oh, God," she whimpers. "Yeah. I want that."

The moment she grabs my shoulders, I shove her tighter to the wall, grip her stupendous arse and lift, so I'm holding her up as she rides me, her sweet pussy spread wide for the taking.

"Shit, shit, watch out," she shrieks which, once I get my tongue back where it belongs, turns to a high, breathless, "Oh, God, oh God, oh God," and, with my next bite, "fuck, Colin. Fuck, fuck, fuck. I want... Oh, God."

I hum against her flesh, actually smiling now.

Can't help it, can I? I've just found the one thing that makes her curse.

CHAPTER ELEVEN

*J*ules

Oh, my God. Oh my God. I'm gonna fall. No, I'm going to suffocate him. No, I'm going to die of the kind of orgasm I've only ever dreamt of.

He's doing things to me that no one's ever done, spearing me deep, lapping me up, wetting his whole face with me. I'd be embarrassed, I think, if I could see him.

Then again, with the way I'm feeling right now, I could forget everything but the pleasure he's giving. And it's not just about friction either, it's about how badly he wants this. How wild it's made him. The sounds he's making of utter desperation.

It feels amazing to be wanted like this.

"Oh, fuck," when his tongue flicks fast against my clit, I lose control of my brain, my mouth. "Fuck, that's good. Don't stop."

He says something, too muffled for me to understand. His arms tighten around my thighs and his body shifts and it feels like excitement. Pure and almost noble, somehow.

Noble? *Noble?* Up here, with my bare ass pressed to cold metal?

Whatever. I'm closer to coming than I've ever been like this—just from a man's tongue and teeth and lips—and I'm not sure the synapses in my brain are snapping the right way. Or connecting. Or...

A moan escapes me, filling the elevator, which is ripe with the smell of sex and metal and scotch, the rumbling of him growling like a beast at the kill. I wind a hand in his hair and tug, hard, and with a snarl, he picks up his pace, pulls me tighter to him, and...

"Holy fucking shit." I curl in on myself, one fist bangs the wall, the other holds his face to me. I shut my eyes tight. And fly.

For a second, the only thing I'm aware of is that hollow metal banging. It's shaking my whole body. Rumbling.

I've never climaxed like this. It's destabilizing. I'm flying and yet, totally in my body, over-sensitive.

I try to close my legs, but he's still there and I'm too limp to push hard, but then the wall behind me's still moving and there's a warm glow all around us, orange through my closed eyelids.

Uh oh.

Oh, crap.

When I pry my eyes open, they hurt. I shut them against the light.

"Colin." I struggle to climb off him, but he only digs

his hands in deeper, heaves me higher on his shoulders and, I'll admit, for a handful of seconds, as I open my eyes to stare down at the top of his dark head, that wide back, those hands, so firm in their control, that I'm tempted to let him keep going. What would be the harm of a second orgasm, right?

But the elevator's not a private place anymore and I can't stare at his windblown hair and the rest of him without also seeing my own pale thighs, spreadeagled around him, and picturing the vision that would greet whoever called the damn thing.

"Colin. We're moving." I don't sound nearly as frenzied as I feel.

He doubles down. I struggle harder. Finally, with an annoyed huff, he tilts his head back and, despite how frantic I am to get off him and throw my shorts on, I'll never forget the way he looks in this moment. Hair tousled, blue eyes hazy, the entire bottom half of his face glistening from what he's just done and his mouth is this ripe, sinful thing. All plump and rosy, almost bruised.

Also, he's a stranger. Not the intimate voice I've spent the last couple hours with, or the warm arms or the frenetic touch.

But, hell, we've got to move or we'll be caught like this.

After another blank second, he gets it, thank God. He's all business. He drops me. Stands, my pink shorts miniscule in his hand. Moves to the call buttons, shoves the garment my way. I'm too busy fighting my way into them to look at what he's up to, so when the elevator comes to an abrupt halt, it takes me a moment to realize that he's holding the doors closed.

I look around, wildly. "What…what floor are we on? Does the door work?"

"Nobody's getting in." I meet his gaze, jarred yet again by this feeling that I don't know him at all. He's not the same. He's a stranger. And also, good lord is he beautiful. "You ready?"

I stand here, confused, lost, caught between our made-up world and this one. No. No, I'm not ready. The second we walk out that door, it's over. I don't want it to end. Shut the light off, lock the door, give me just one more minute in the dark, cocooned safety of his arms.

"Ready."

"Let's go." With a grin, he turns, slides the doors wide, throws open the outer one, and then stops abruptly. "What the—"

I bump into him with an audible *oof*.

"Hello you creepy little fucker."

I follow his gaze down and realize with a jolt that he's staring at Madame Christen's brown and white terrier. It's staring up at us, ears at half mast, head tilted at a curious angle. Its eyes are two black beads reflecting the elevator's yellow light.

"What floor are we on?" I whisper, shrinking back under the dog's steady stare.

"Second," he replies under his breath.

"Did you push the button for this floor?"

He shakes his head, caught in a staring contest with the beast. "Pushed three. And zero."

"Oh my God."

"Chouchou!" Madame Christen's voice wails out from her cracked apartment door. "Viens, mon p'tit bichounet. Il fait froid là!"

"Jesus," Colin whispers. And then to the dog, "Thanks, buddy. Owe you one." After giving Chouchou a quick scratch behind the ear, he turns back to scoop up my shoes and the bottle, grabs my hand, and we make a break for the stairs.

I stifle my laughter until the fourth floor, but once I let it out, it's awfully close to hysterical. "What the hell was that? Did I imagine it?"

"No, you did not. The devil dog saved us."

"You don't actually think Chouchou pushed the button, do you?"

His expression says he's definitely not ruling the possibility out. "That dog is getting steaks for life."

I want that, I think absurdly. Only not steak, but… What? What do I want for life? Something panicky flutters in my chest as Colin moves up the last flight to his floor at a more sedate pace. Ridiculously, I want to pull back on his hand and slow him even more.

Hey! Let's stay out here on the stairs or, better yet, go back into our freezing, dark elevator.

"What should…" The question fizzles in my mouth. *What should we do now?* I'd been about to ask, but I'm suddenly afraid of the answer.

He looks hard, in the stark hallway light. His eyes are sharp, his mouth flat. The lost, soft, sensual thing we've just shared is gone. Was it even real?

He's holding my hand and his coat is on my shoulders. I'm carrying my shoes and the half-finished bottle. These are all that's left of the time we spent in that box together.

And I hate it. I want the box back, despite being desperate to pee. And I really, really need some water. And I'm starving, actually.

Although that thing eating at my insides might not be hunger so much as pain at the idea of never meeting my elevator man again. I want him back, the way he was. I want us back. I want...

We get to his floor and I put on a smile, reach for my shoes, and internally practice the right kind of friendly goodbye for the occasion.

It hurts, I'll admit, but I'm leaving in two days. It'll be easier to rip off the bandage if we don't linger.

He starts. "So, uh—"

"Here." I yank off his coat, immediately cold. "Thank you. You are—"

"Perhaps we—"

I stop, breath held.

He stops. "Go on."

"No, it's just that..." I shrug, feeling lame and lost and slightly embarrassed now that he's this beautiful, intimidating man again and I'm just...me.

"You need to check your oven?" It's the perfect out. A ready-made excuse to rush up there and hide. Quiet as a mouse.

"Yes," I say. "Right. Better do that."

He nods. "You got your keys?"

"Yep." I pat my hoodie pocket, avoiding his eyes. I

don't know what makes me add, "Would you like an eggnog?"

His face wrinkles up into its usual look of annoyance. "Isn't that the custard you Americans drink like milk?"

"I guess so. Never mind. Better go use the...the loo." I force a smile, hating how awkward it all suddenly feels. "Thank you for, um, everything."

Trying hard to hide the hurt at his lack of response —why would I hurt anyway, right?—I turn and race up the stairs.

COLIN

It's shocking how quickly the world's turned inside out. Or upside down or whatever the fuck's happened to my insides. Walking into that lift was like boarding the bloody TARDIS, except instead of changing the time or place, it changed *me*.

Now, I'm stuck in a stunned state of stasis—which reminds me of something The Doctor might say—and, rather than race after her, the way every muscle in my body is screaming at me to do, all I manage is to watch her little blue painted toes disappear up the steps. I listen to the rattle of her keys and the opening and closing of her door. Then, like the pathetic half man I am, I stalk into my own flat, shut my door, and just listen.

Is she being extra quiet now, in an effort to...what?

Get space from me? Hide? Maintain some level of privacy, perhaps?

That would make sense, I suppose.

I turn on a light and flip on my telly, out of habit, then come to a stop and take in my flat with fresh eyes.

It's serviceable. Boring, really. The cheapest sofa, the cheapest table, chairs. The telly's where I put a bit more cash. And the sound system. They're the only two things that matter, aside from the pub, though now that I think of it, none of those things matter to me in the slightest.

The telly's home screen is up, giving me all the options and I can't think of a single fucking thing I'd watch right now. Not one.

I notice the coat on my arm and press the warm inside to my face. I smell her sweetness, still taste her on my mouth.

I plug my phone in and wash my hands, all the while listening for her, all the while disappointed.

I've been home for maybe three minutes, when the floor creaks above.

Standing in the middle of my lounge, I go completely still, listening harder than I ever have in my life. I want the sound of her voice, that fucking laugh. I'd do anything to hear it now.

The way I'd do anything to talk to Eddie just one more time. To show him our pub, pour him a pint, share just that with him.

I can't have my brother back. He's gone. Forever.

Another board creaks above. I try to picture her in what I've seen of her flat. It's bright and colorful, full of light in the morning.

My head tilts back. I stare at my ceiling, willing her to take another step, shift the floorboard, let out a laugh, make a nuisance of herself however she bloody well likes.

What if, instead of standing here like a wanker, I went up there, right now, and did my best to win her— that miracle of a woman who shook up my entire existence tonight? What if…

Fuck it.

Just before leaving, I grab the whisky. The night's not over until we've finished the bottle, I recklessly decide. A second before shutting my door, I turn around and go back in for one more thing.

CHAPTER TWELVE

*J*ules

My stomach hurts. My throat's tight. I feel... I don't know. This isn't regret. At least I don't think so.

I checked the oven. It was off. I'm in the tiny bathroom, about to turn on the shower, when there's a knock at my door.

It's probably Colin. Though I know this, I cycle through a series of unlikely possibilities. Is it Madame Christen's dog playing ding-dong ditch with the neighbors? It could also be Colin here to return something to me. Or maybe he needs to borrow a cup of sugar or coffee or probably his WiFi's out and he needs my password so he can watch some slasher flick.

I throw on my fuzzy robe as I walk to the door, suck in a deep, nervous breath, and throw it open.

Just seeing him standing there makes me nauseous. It's the upside down version of this morning.

"Hey," I force out between stiff lips.

He watches me, then seems to steel himself and holds up the bottle we shared. "I reckon this might go well in eggnog. Not sure, as I've never tried the stuff. Are you still planning on making some?"

"No." My tone is as flat as I feel.

"Yeah. I didn't really want it any way."

His hair's dark, his cheekbones wide, the stubble on his jaw looks rougher than it feels and, like a starving person, all I want is to drink in the sight of him. Every detail. The way his jeans fit those thick thighs, the way his eyes darken as they take me in. Connecting with that stare head-on zaps me back to reality.

"What…um… What was it you wanted, then?"

His gaze on mine is as solid as the elevator's metal wall against my back. The connection resonates in my bones. I can't look away.

"You, Jules. I want you."

It's unclear who moves first. Him, I think. It's almost frightening how fast our bodies come together. There'll be bruises from this.

The way he watches me as our lips meet, my God, I feel that as surely as the hot press of his mouth covering mine, urging mine open, our tongues sliding and tasting and taking. Getting to use our eyes on each other has opened up a whole new world.

I stumble back, him with me, his arms supporting the dangerous moving object we've become. Bashing into a side table, knocking my keys to the floor. My gaze eats up every part of him. His throat, his shoulders, the tiny freckles I had no idea were there. He kicks the door closed and it takes every functioning brain cell I've got to make sure we don't smash the place as we careen on, eyes much too busy taking each other in to worry about the rest of the universe.

Finally, the kitchen island stops our advance.

I'm not sure he even notices, except that it's a surface to put his bottle on.

And then to put me on. I'm heaved up and my robe's pulled open and everything stops.

"Holy shit," he whispers, his face blank as his eyes rove over my body.

I know, it's a lot to take in. I'm all breasts and belly, white flesh usually lifted, locked, and loaded in underwire bras and well-fitted skirts. He's getting an eyeful and if he doesn't like it, well he can leave, because I'm good with what I've got and—

"Glorious," he whispers, like he's just gotten back the ability to speak. "Fucking beautiful. Look. Look at your pretty tits, love. Look at all this…" With a kind of reverence, he drops his head and kisses the crook of my neck.

I've never *felt* myself being looked at before. Not like this. His reverence is a caress. The skim of his gaze sets off a mad series of goosebumps.

Slowly, he drags the robe off my shoulder, his lips trailing behind his fingers, leaving pure fire in their wake. As his hot mouth scores a downward path over my skin, he hums a sound of pleasure and pain. He gets to my breasts and steps back, his mouth dropping open as if he can't handle the awe running through him. *Seeing* so much on his face is almost frightening after all the sounds and tastes and smells we shared. It's almost too much.

"Fucking hell, love. I need…"

"What?" I watch him closely, my vision blurring at the edges. *Definitely* too much.

"I'll need every minute you've got left just to play with these gorgeous tits." Slowly, he strokes the backs of his knuckles against my breasts—the sides, underneath —finally cupping and weighing them with a groan of hedonistic pleasure.

His knuckles catch one swollen nipple in a quick, tight pinch before moving to the other, his eyes following his handiwork with avid fascination. So much to look at. So much to see. I'm throbbing with every touch, every flicker of those eyes. It's overwhelming how all of our senses work together at once.

"You're my fucking fantasy come to life." A hard pinch that makes me gasp, followed by a tender caress. "I'll be needing so much more, though, now that I've tasted your sweet little pussy."

Oh my God, the man talks dirty.

"I'm going to fuck you so hard, Jules."

At his words, I lose my ability to speak. To think.

Colin, however, does not. "You know how many times I've thought about this gorgeous body? This mouth?" He dips and plucks at my lips with his.

With a wicked grin, he bends lower and takes my nipple between his teeth. After lashing me with his tongue, he pulls back to look closely at how glossy he's made me and a thread inside me snaps.

"Okay, then." I'm an animal, moaning and wiggling to get him closer. "Do it!"

He goes back in to suck and pull, grips my other

breast with rough efficiency, then switches and...oh, God. I go rigid, my face screwed up tight, my entire body tied in knots from so much sensation.

The sights and sounds and pleasure and pain all come together into a sharp point inside me, acute, almost unbearable. When I remember to open my eyes, I see my hands on his head, holding him to my chest. My mouth's begging wordlessly for more.

Could I come from this?

Probably not.

But I'm twisting and squirming and working hard to get friction with his lower half and, try as I might, it's too damn far. I reach forward to tug at his shirt.

He ignores me as he descends into sucking and biting, with needy grunts that seem so different from the man I'd thought he was, it's like I've stepped into a new reality. Behind a mirror, looking outward. The same scene, but reversed. Not an uptight asshole, but a sensitive man in pain. A man who's never learned to love or be loved. A man carrying so much guilt on his shoulders that he's left room for nothing else.

But then I think of how he'd carried my weight on his shoulders earlier and a shudder of want runs through me. I force myself out of my own cloud of arousal and reach for his jeans. The top button's easy to pry open, but with his head bent over my breasts, I can't reach the zipper. I try to nudge him away with an impatient "My turn."

"No. First, I need..."

What? What does he need? Because I need his mouth and his hands and his cock and I need them fast and hard. I need to soak up every bit of him with my eyes. This slow worship thing is amazing, but we've spent the last three hours cooped up in an elevator, not daring, not doing, and now I want it all.

"Take it off," I demand, bossier than I intend. "God, please just do it. I'm dying, Colin. I feel—"

He bites me and I yelp as, with a rough little laugh, he steps back and pulls his henley off, then the T-shirt underneath.

I go stock still at the sight of him. I was already excited, already wet and so into this man, but seeing him like this—solid and ready and gorgeous—has stalled me out.

How could I have forgotten how beautiful he is? Just this morning, I had this same view—minus one rather significant detail—but it's like I'm seeing him all over again. And, in a way, I guess I am.

I love that he's not lean and carved out like some of the guys I've been with, but thick, bulky, solid. He looks strong and capable. He pinches my nipples, my eyes slide down, and my jaw drops. A primal thrill runs through me, part excitement, part fear.

The man's cock is *huge.*

I know this because the fat, glossy crown is visible just below his belly button, a single drop of fluid pearled at the tip. And it's not just long, it's thick and plump and what I see of it is absolutely gorgeous. "Holy crap, Colin."

He steps away and glances down at himself, his usually stern face flushed and tight and possibly a tiny bit worried. "What. You alri'?" That last word emerges

105

with a little roll of the R. It must be a Welsh thing. I love it. And I'll definitely pay more attention to it when I can rip my gaze from his dick. "Is it my cock?" How does he sound actually worried?

I mean, he maybe has reason to be. I've got no idea how to deal with a monster like that. "It's big," I admit, staring as the bead swells and rolls down the side, just begging to be lapped up with my tongue. "But I'm willing to try."

"Fuck. My sweet, dirty girl"

"Also just realized that I'm not the only one who's been going commando."

"Told you I don't wear pants."

Right. No pants. I look at him now with a sort of awe that, from that first awful exchange, we've somehow made it to this point.

His face breaks into a grin and all those feelings I had earlier in the safety of the dark come rocketing back, only they're not dreamlike and weirdly half drunk now, they're a solid, sober hit to the sternum.

I don't know him that well, but I... God, I feel so much for him. Lust, yeah, a hundred times yes, and so much more than that.

"You're scaring me, love. What is it?"

"I like you," I tell him, the words whispered and worried. "A lot."

He nods, watching me closely, face serious. "I like you, too."

"It's..."

"Scary as fuck."

A laugh bursts out of me. "Yeah. So scary."

"That's all right, baby." His expression goes solemn and earnest as he comes in and puts a hand to my face. "It'll only hurt a little going in."

I snort-laugh and smack his arm and he grins and leans in and kisses me again and, this time, I *know* he likes me. And I like him. And we want each other. There's safety in all of that. Need, too, but not the same edgy thing we'd experienced before.

Sharing a laugh will do that, I guess. Telling the truth, too.

He pulls out of the kiss slowly, our lips separating with a light smack. When I open my eyes, I find him watching me, his wide, dry palm cradling the side of my face, his expression tender and a little shocked.

"All right, then," he whispers against me before inhaling, slow and deep. "Now, love, are you going to take this cock like a good girl, or do I have to get you back inside that lift and turn the lights out?"

And, just like that, it's on.

CHAPTER THIRTEEN

*C*olin
 When she doesn't answer, I go still.

All right. She doesn't like it. I'd not thought that far ahead, obviously, but sadly, I'm not a prince in the sack. I'm a beast. That's a fact that I've admitted to every woman I've ever been with. I don't do pretty words or poetry. I don't do affection or romance at all. I'm a little rough, a little hard, and entirely clear on what I like. My partners know this, they accept it, they like it, too, or they don't do it at all. And that's fine by me.

Usually.

But I've never laughed with a woman before. And I've never wanted to keep one this badly.

Our closeness should scare me, yet it doesn't.

However, if she's not into rough and hard, then I'm fucked. And not in a good way.

"Tell me," I say, my voice going low and mean, showing her how I'll be once I'm inside her. From her spot on the counter, she watches me, her eyes big, her pupils blown wide open. "Tell me you want this cock. I can give you hard and dirty. I don't do the rest, love. Not the pretty words or the frilly bits. Will you take what I have to give you?"

A slow smile spreads over her tiny, plump mouth and relief flows through me, spiking hard when she says, "Like a good girl."

"Oh, fuck, that's exactly what you are. You're a good girl." I smile and she grins wide and now, the only thing I'll worry about, once I've retrieved my brain cells from my balls, is how the hell I'll get this magical woman to stay.

Preferably right here, seated on the kitchen counter, only with my cock deep inside her.

"Better warn you," I say. "I'm a bossy fucker."

She snorts again, the sound gloriously uninhibited. "Yeah. Now, there's the real shocker."

With a smile, I put my hand on her knee and push her legs open, all the while watching her reaction. It's gratifying. Mouth open, eyes half closed, breathing choppy.

"I've got a condom." Or twelve.

"I have some, too."

My rush of jealous anger is absurd, though undeniable, and rather than try to repress it, I let it rev me up. "You've had a lot of lovers here, then?"

"Have you?" Her eyes flick up to meet mine.

"No."

"Me neither." Now it's her turn to smile. "Besides, you'd have heard if I did."

"Touché." I push the breath up and out, and let my gaze enjoy her body while fully unzipping my jeans.

She makes an uncomfortable sound—half moan, half protest. I don't care. I've finally got the chance to look her over and I'll fucking do it in my own good time. "Stop squirming, gorgeous girl. Be good while I get ready."

The way she moves shows just how much she enjoys the things coming from my mouth. Thank fucking God. What would I have done if she'd turned out to be prim and proper and preferred missionary in the dark?

I skate a hand down her side, taking in freckles and bumps with my fingers and eyes. After all our time spent in the dark, it's a treat just to look at her. She's got dimples on her arse and thighs. But I already knew that. Bless those short, flouncy skirts.

"You're so fucking soft, Jules. All these curves, so lush, begging to be taken. And blimey, this beautiful cunt." I shove my trousers down, push her legs wider, and soak up the view, priming my hard prick with one hand while the other spreads her lips wide open so my eyes can fully feast. "Fuck, love, I've got to taste you again or I'll—"

It's impossible to finish the sentence once my mouth lands on her hot, fragrant pussy. After a long, slow lick, I pull back and meet her eyes over the luxuriant landscape of her body. "You're soaked again."

Her face goes red—embarrassed? Turned on?—and I lick her deep, keeping our gazes locked, tight and intense. This pussy is mine, I decide, using my nose to spread her lips before flicking her clit with my tongue. Even if she doesn't yet realize it.

This woman, her smell, her looks, that evil little sense of humor, even the off-key humming and the chicken laugh. I want all of it. Constantly.

"Colin, please. I need you inside me," she finally says and, that admission, though tame in comparison with some of the things we've said tonight, sends me.

I bend and root around in my trouser pockets. A handful of condoms spill out onto the floor. I snag one, rip it open with my teeth, and roll it onto my erection in record time. All the while, she stares at my throbbing cock, her expression equal parts intimidated and excited.

I'm pounding with want as I step up and slide my cockhead through her slippery softness. "Lie back." I grin, planting a kiss on her mouth. "And hold on."

With a nervous laugh, she complies. For a half second, I can do nothing but stare at how she's offered herself up to me, spread out on the kitchen counter.

Then I wrap an arm around her thigh, notch myself to that gorgeous little place I tongue-fucked with so much gusto, and press inside.

The first centimeter's enough to make me throw my head back. After a moment, I get a grip on myself, tighten my hold, and tug her closer, leaning to give her just the slightest bit of weight at the same time.

"Oh, fucking hell, you're tight."

My eyes shut and I breathe through the unbearable pleasure of piercing this woman's flesh with mine. Caught behind closed eyelids, we're in the dark lift again, cut off from the world. The two of us nothing but voices, bodies, smells.

My composure cracks. I open my eyes, let the light in, the sight of her not helping me keep my cool in the least.

I work hard to get back control of my senses, let myself look down, and feast on the sight of us. It's perfectly filthy the way I split her open with every press of my hips to hers. When the stretch becomes unbearably tight, I lean over, put a hand to her tit, my thumb to her clit, and play her like an instrument made just for me.

Immediately, she becomes a vise. Another flick of my thumb and she loosens. I thrust harder, moving her body on the counter, jiggling her tits, pushing a high gasp from her mouth. "That's it, love. Take it. Take this fucking cock. Christ, look at you, all laid out like a feast. I want to…"

Her moaned response hits me low, in the balls and, rather than take my time the way I have been, my hands move to her hips and my short-circuiting body jerks her onto me.

Finally I'm in, bottoming out, blessedly, completely. "Fuck, your cunt's fucking perfect." With her next needy sound, I pull back and slam inside, my vision overcome with something greedy and dark. Another slam. Another. "How do you want it?"

She lifts her head and looks at me, our connection scarily palpable. "I want what you'll give me. I want it all."

"Don't say that. You don't know."

"I want to be yours," she gasps, pulling the thought straight from my head. "Do what you want to me. Make this yours. Take it. Yours."

"God yes," I gasp, powering inside her now, with none of my usual caution. The only part of me that's not selfish is that thumb, tweaking her clit with every thrust. "Mine."

"Yours, Colin. Yours."

Another pump, explicit and slow enough to send tingles rushing to the base of my spine. "Do that again. Say it."

"Yours."

"My name."

"Colin."

I nod, grunting like an animal, fucking into her hard and fast and frantic. "You need to come, love. Come all over this cock. Come on it, squeeze it all out of me." My mouth's got a mind of its own now, dark and filthy and rough. "Fuck, I want to fill you."

Images flash before my eyes—these tits ripe and dark, her belly massive and hard. I screw my eyes shut and try to shove it away, but more comes—my come dripping from her, my fingers and cock and tongue pressing it back inside, making her keep it, making her body keep it.

Shit, this is hot. And probably way too much for her, but I'm mindless now, my thighs burning, my cock going thicker, harder, the need to blow turning me into something monstrous, hungry, a little wrong. Or a lot.

"I want to fuck you bare," I tell her, shocking myself. "I want to feel your skin against mine, raw, real."

"Colin. Yeah. Yes. That's good." She's scrabbling for a hold, her fingers scratching my arms, my arse when she can grasp it. "I want that. I need that, too. Fill me up."

Her words are explosive. My body's gone haywire, my hips too fast, my hands clutching, kneading, for her pleasure. I hope. I'm chaos. It's all chaos. My brain, my muscles, the way the words tumble out: dark admissions from the abyss of my soul.

"I want to keep you, Jules. Strap you to this table. Keep you open and waiting. I want to use you like this, let you use me. Over and over, until we've both had enough."

"Oh, God." Her voice has edged up into a whine. "Oh, no. I'm coming. Colin, you've got to…"

Her pussy clenches, spasming round my cock. She shudders, tightens, her hands grasping tight at my arms, scratching, the movement as thoughtless and wild as the heavy slap of my balls against her.

"Colin," she screams, her gaze on me as she goes under and I'm close. Fuck, so close.

"This is mine, isn't it?" I slam deep. Slam home.

"Yours," she whispers, her head thrown back, her chest heaving. She's so tight I can barely move, but it's enough. It's enough.

Then, through pained-sounding vocal cords, she says my name one last time.

"*Colin.*"

That's it. I'm gone.

Electricity shoots down my spine to my balls and while my mouth pours out words I can no longer keep track of, my cock pulses with the first hot jet of my release. It's almost painful to shut my eyes on the sight of her body, but I can't keep them open. Can't handle more than one sensation as I experience the longest, most powerful orgasm of my life.

Halfway through, I say something I know I'll regret.

I'm so gone, I don't even care.

CHAPTER FOURTEEN

*J*ules

"Don't go."

I'm still floating when he says it, but now it's here, in the air above me, settling on my skin.

Unless I imagined it, which I'm almost sure of until he says more.

"Stay."

One word, but it's big. It feels like more than four letters. Big enough to fill up my chest.

His hands grip my hips and inside me he convulses with an orgasm that looks as intense as mine was. From the look on his face, I'd say maybe more.

I want to kiss that hard mouth, that tense jaw. I want to run my hands through his wild hair, over the shoulders whose heft shouldn't have to carry all the weight he drags around with him every day.

He's a big, strong man, I know, but he's mortal, too. A human, crumbling under too much sadness, guilt, loss and probably a good dose of toxic masculinity to boot.

My body shudders with a delayed reaction to that climax, which was above and beyond anything it's been put through before. I mean, it was good. Amazing. And also almost scary in how hard it hit me. From the inside, exploding out.

Gratitude, or something like it, wells up beside the other stuff that's prematurely raised its too-tender head. As I watch him, waiting for his eyes to open and his fists to unclench and for something other than that grim, gritted-teeth look on his face to appear, the endorphins fizzle out and the cold counter I'm lying on registers and I start to wonder if we've pried ourselves open too wide, let too much spill out in such a short time.

With a final squeeze, he releases the air he's apparently been holding, along with all that tension. Then he opens his eyes with what looks exactly like happiness and something unlatches inside of me and my chest gets all squirrely and...

No. No, no, no. I don't want this. I don't want these feelings. Not now. Not right when I'm leaving, when responsibility's calling me away and every one of my instincts is telling me to go. Get out while I can. Before this place and this man get their claws into me. Before it hurts.

In the silence, a smile breaks out on his face and it's soul-crushingly sweet. He looks so *young*. And here I am, with his thick, still-hard erection deep inside me, thinking of running away.

I shut my eyes and swallow back the panic and guilt.

I'm not running. That's not what I do. What I do is travel, discover, expand my horizons. What I do is move

117

forward, take in more and more and more. It's not avoidance if you're running *towards* the next thing.

When I look at him again, the smile's gone, his expression's quizzical.

"You alri'?" That little contraction, or whatever you call it when a word's cut off, is nothing like the rest of him.

Except for that smile.

Yeah, well the smile was a fluke. The man is big and hard and a loner and that's the way it should be. For both of us.

Only, I know that's not true. I feel shame just thinking it, about him, at least. He's no loner. He's a man who's been hurt and needs...something.

Whatever it is, I'm not the one to give it. I'm not the person to help or heal or be a part of any of it.

I can't...I can't...

"You've gone off someplace, haven't you?" With a sigh, he slowly pulls out, leaving me empty and bereft, with a strong desire to cry.

And I don't cry. Ever.

"Don't do that, love. I'm not... It was just words, all right? Just words. I'm not trying to..." Now, the smile he gives me is sad and I *did* that. I am absolutely responsible for that look.

I hate myself for it.

"I'm good," I lie, pushing up to sitting with a grimace.

"Shit. Was I too rough? I know I can be—"

"You were perfect." I grab his arm and drag my hand down to clasp his. "I'm a little sore. I mean, you are *huge*, mister."

He groans and looks down at where his deflating cock's still wearing the condom.

I shiver at the memory of his words. *I want to fuck you bare. I want to feel your skin against mine, raw, real.*

It's too much. Not just horny, but somehow stark and human and real in a way that I can't stand to think about.

Imagine baring yourself like that. No armor, no skin to protect you.

I glance away. "But I'm good. I feel *great*, actually." As if to compound the lie, I grin hard and stretch my arms wide and wiggle my eyebrows at him. I'm a hairsbreadth from doing jazz hands when I realize I should probably rein it in.

Thankfully, he's too busy tying off the condom to pay any attention to my theatrics. This also gives me a chance to hop to the floor and slip back into my robe. I open the trash for him and give him another fake, bright smile, wishing I felt light inside, instead of heavy.

Though the urge to watch him pull himself back together again is strong, I deny it. It seems wrong, suddenly, to enjoy any part of this, when it's got to end. It *has* to. It shouldn't have even started, this weird thing between us. Instead, I pick up the bottle of wine I started earlier tonight—what feels like a lifetime ago—and attempt to shove the too-wide cork back into the opening, without success.

"You seem..." I look up to catch him watching me, narrow-eyed and cautious. "Are you all right? You sure I didn't—"

"I'm good, but I should, um..." God, why can't I get

119

this cork in? It came out, right? I should be able to shove the stupid thing back into the neck, which has somehow shrunk down to the size of a pinhole. I point a thumb toward the bedroom, not for one second letting myself picture him sprawled out in sleep or smiling at me from heavy-lidded morning eyes, his face lined from his pillow. *My* pillow. I can't have those things. Those are everyday things and I don't do everyday. I slam at the cork, my palm skidding off. I can't do everyday. If I do, I'll—

"Jules." He steps up, takes the bottle from me and, without apparent effort, tucks the cork inside. "Jules, love."

I know it's a common endearment, but the word singes my skin.

"Jules." He stands in front of me and leans down to meet my eyes, his expression one of concern. "You all right?"

I swallow back an unwelcome rush of emotion and force another big, fake smile to my face. "Great. Thank you for, uh… That was nice."

At his frown, I see that I've made a strategic error, but it's too late. I'm on this path and I can't stop myself.

"Nice?" He huffs out a sound of disbelief. "Nothing about that was nice. It was many things, but not nice. Remember what you said in the lift?"

"What I said?"

"That thing about how it felt fated to you? Us getting stuck together. *Important.* That's the word you used."

Did I say that? Crap, I think I did. It comes back to

me in a rush. "You disagreed. And rightly so. Fate's not a thing. It's a construct, a—"

"What if, though? What if Fate or Karma or the Ghost of bloody Christmas decided to give us a chance at something real? Then who the hell are we to deny it?" He shakes his head, his eyes burning with something fierce and alive. "I'm going to bloody well grab this opportunity by the balls. And I'm taking you with me, you miracle of a woman."

My mouth opens and closes a few times, but nothing comes out. My mind's a perfect, stunned blank.

"Nice?" I've got no idea what he's thinking as he looks me over now, shaking his head. "You want to pretend it was *nice?*" After a long, heavy sigh, he appears to come to some decision. He leans forward and plants a kiss on my forehead. "If that's how you'd like to play it. I'll let it go." He heads for the door, which he opens and steps through. He's on the threshold when he turns, looking almost as mean as the first time I saw him. Then, in the most threatening voice I've ever heard, he warns, "For now," and disappears, his footsteps heavy on the stairs.

I'm left standing here, stunned and lonely and shell-shocked, with no idea what will happen next.

CHAPTER FIFTEEN

*C*olin

    Nice. *Nice?* What a laugh.

I storm down the steps to my flat.

I get it. I do. I see what she's doing, how she thinks she's somehow putting things right after the lift came and shook it all up.

I know better, though. Now. I know divine intervention when I see it. Feel it. Live it. And I know she did, too.

She fucking said it, didn't she? She told me, flat out, that we were living something special and she's right. I denied it, to her face. I told her fate had nothing to do with it. Told her attraction was all it was.

I see now that I was a liar. Or at the very least, a fool. Who did I think I was to refuse the gift of fate, or whatever's been pulling these strings? I'm done with that now, aren't I? I'm ready to move on. Ready to live, not just survive.

Thank Christ I can be a stubborn bastard when it's called for.

I'm driven, I've got no limits, my ethics are questionable at best. Or at least, the old me was all those things. The new me… Well, I'm a work in progress.

First, before anything else, I'm heading out in search of Christmas. It'll be a right pain in the arse, given how dead Paris is at this ungodly hour, but there's bound to be someone with something to spare. And I'll bloody well find it.

I'm ready to believe in miracles.

* * *

JULES

After he leaves, I stumble to the shower and brush my teeth, avoiding my own image in the mirror.

You miracle of a woman.

Why would he say that? Why would he think it? It was the sex talking. That's all.

I grab my phone and head toward bed.

Solène's bed. A bed that's been very comfy these past three months. But it's not mine. I don't have a bed.

Up until now, that's been exactly the way I've wanted it. Who wants to be shackled by a home and a job and too many belongings? Who needs one of those relationships that quickly turns into a prison?

I think of Enora across the hall and the guy she's been seeing and how his very fancy French family talks down to her and she takes it—for his sake.

And the worst part, the very worst, is that he's not

worth it at all. He's the kind of dick you bump into at a party and his hand somehow lands on your ass and when you say something about it, you're treated like the paranoid one. A professional gaslighter.

Ask me how I know.

Sighing, I shove the covers up and out of the way and tiptoe to the window overlooking the cute little pedestrian square below. I can't see Colin's pub from here, since it's six flights down, directly under where I'm standing. I can, however, see the Christmas lights lining the cobblestoned alley and the flicker of rain or sleet or whatever it is currently falling from the sky.

My vision blurs and, at first, I think it's from droplets on the window, but after a few blinks, it occurs to me that I've got tears in my eyes, which is so rare I almost can't believe it.

God, how many times have I wished I could cry? The pain wells up, along with the loneliness and the feeling of missing Mom *so hard* and then right behind it, the realization that I didn't even know her, really, and that she never got the chance to know the adult I've become.

The fact that the tears have chosen tonight, of all nights, to overflow is incomprehensible to me.

Why? Why do I care about any of this?

I love Paris, yes, but it's not like it loves me back. I've had great food here, yes. Made a wonderful friend and now had great sex, but that's not enough to keep me in this place. Is it?

Is it?

Great sex.

My forehead thunks against the cold glass and my vision goes totally blurry until I have to shut my eyes to squeeze the tears out and it's only the sound of a door slamming somewhere below that drags me out of this sappy mire of emotion.

It's Christmas doing this to me. And the late night. And feeling like a hamster on a wheel of my own creation.

But I like my wheel.

Don't I?

My mind skips over the next few months. I'll be in Milan and then Athens and then I don't know. Someplace else. Busy. Different. Fun!

I blink out at a lone figure walking down the alley, just a dark silhouette hunched against the cold. I shiver just thinking of how freezing it must be out there and that makes me think of the bone-deep chill in the elevator. And then how hot it got once we touched.

There'd also been the still and the quiet.

The closeness.

I don't think I ever felt that before tonight.

A tear escapes the corner of my eye and slides down my cheek and, rather than sit here questioning everything that I am, I pull the curtain closed on the city's eerie pink light and crawl back into bed.

Tomorrow, I won't feel this weight on my chest. Tomorrow, it'll be ancient history. Or a dream.

I wish that didn't make me feel so sad.

CHAPTER SIXTEEN

*C*olin

An hour later, I'm standing in the Place de la Bastille, out of breath and hope.

I stare up at the Colonne de Juillet, the Génie de la Liberté statue floating atop it, all tarted up in fresh gold, with its tiny todger and wide wings, the whole thing tipped with an actual bloody star, like the Christmas tree I still haven't managed to locate.

It shouldn't be that hard, should it? Finding a tree? I know I've never once tried and I'm ridiculously late, given that it's now four o'clock on Christmas morning, but the fated miracle feeling tricked me into thinking—

"Eh, qu'est-ce que tu fous là, toi?" A familiar voice asks me what I'm doing here.

I turn and see Raf, the man who sells chestnuts outside my pub. I can't believe I saw him just last evening. Feels as though a lifetime has passed between the two.

"T'es perdu?"

I shake my head. "Not lost. Just…found myself too late, I suppose."

Raf, being French and a pragmatic man to begin with, doesn't bother asking what the hell I'm going on about or whether I've lost more than my sense of self in the last few hours. Instead, he looks pointedly around us at the empty roads, the darkened brasseries, and shuttered shops, their Christmas lights still twinkling cruelly from within. "Trop tard? No, it's never too late, my friend. Not in Paris. Not tonight. Do you need help?"

Not believing for a moment that we'll find it, I tell him what I'd hoped to do. He nods at a pile of electric scooters, dumped a few meters away. "Can you rent us a couple of those?"

I nod, pulling up the app.

"Come on, then."

Our first stop is only three blocks from my pub. And it's the most important one. Raf, who apparently knows everything that happens here, leads me down an alley and through a gate that hasn't quite latched and there, lying in an interior courtyard, as if tossed to the cobblestones from a flat above, is a poor, sad lump of a pine tree, clothed in nothing but its needles.

"There it is." He points at the poor, denuded tree. "All yours."

"You're sure they're not coming back to get it?" I eye the darkened windows above.

"Non." His head shake is categorical. "She moved out." He grins. "And he's a complete shit. Doesn't deserve a tree." He shrugs. "Or a wife."

"How do you know all this?" I ask, hefting the thing and heading in the direction of the scooters we left at the entrance.

"Sound echoes in the night." He points back toward the courtyard. "I watched her take the kids and run yesterday." Even in the dark, I see the flash of his teeth. "I may or may not have blocked his pursuit."

I bark out a surprised laugh, wondering if all this time, he hasn't been the one watching out for me, instead of the other way around.

We run the tree back to the pub, where I use a red plastic bucket to set it upright, and then back out for more supplies. Bolstered by this first success, I send texts, calling in favors with people all over the city.

It takes ages to gather most of what we need and, on the scooters, the job is difficult, but there's freedom to riding around with the wind in my face, no cars or honking or pedestrians in the way. Just the wet pavement and Raf and fairy lights *everywhere*.

Hours later, I stand inside the pub and look around, stunned, at the decorations and festive atmosphere we've created in such a short time. The pilfered Christmas tree, now draped in tinsel, twinkles brightly in the window, which has been painted in the kind of cozy nordic snowscape that always annoyed me in the past, but somehow now just makes me feel like I'm in the right place.

No matter what happens.

For possibly the fiftieth time tonight—today?—Raf sing/shouts the chorus from *Petit Papa Noël*, one of the better known French Christmas songs, joined by his friend Annette and her boyfriend, Hervé, who recently bought one of the old bouquiniste book stalls along the Seine, and then Rémy, who's come in to watch Rugby a few times. He's a florist on l'Île de la Cité, it turns out. And lucky for me, there's always extra around Christmas.

Tonight's been eye-opening, actually. Between Raf's friends and a few of my customers—friends, too, I suppose—and other business owners whom I'd never have thought to contact for myself, we've brought together quite the network. I'd not considered these people anything more than acquaintances before, but they've helped, quite happily.

This generosity, along with everything that's happened tonight, has blown me away.

I've changed.

Miracles, I reckon, looking at the crew now heading back out into the night, are real. Some we build with our own hands—and the help of others—and some are gifts from...providence? The world?

Fate?

After they've all gone off to their various dwellings, Raf and I step back and eye our handiwork one last time. Something like pride swells inside me and then I realize that it's not pride at all. This is different. I've felt pride and it's a cold, empty thing. This emotion is warm and so full, I'm overflowing with it.

"Merci," I say to the man. He reaches out to shake my hand and, instead I step in and put my arms around him and hug him hard, my eyes shut tight to keep the feelings from overflowing. "*Merci.*"

When I pull away, there's as much of a shine in his eyes as in mine. I turn and cough in my hand. I now smell of smoke and chestnuts and probably a healthy dose of car fumes.

"Come on up," I say. "Have a wash. Sleep in a bed." I cast a look at the quiet cobbled alley. "No one's clamoring for chestnuts out here. Come. Let me thank you for all that you've done."

"Where will you sleep?" he asks and the fact that this man whose struggles are harsh and real worries about me missing a single night in my bed...well, it hits me so hard it feels like pain.

And maybe it is pain, this rush of feeling. But I can take it. I'm strong enough now that I've gained this bit of perspective. Strength, I see after those hours with an angel in the dark, isn't about being hard or tough or taking one for the team. Strength is letting everything in and giving it a home. The sadness, the loss, the aches and pains of lives lived and lost. All of it makes us who we are.

"This pub's for my brother, you know," I say, apropos of absolutely nothing.

"Yeah?"

"Yes." I point at the painted letters curving above the door. "Iorwerth. It's Welsh for Edward."

"That's his name?"

Was, I almost correct him. "Yes," I say instead. "Yes, that's his name."

"It's a good name, Colin. Unlike yours." He grins wide, shaking his head. "Who on earth names their kid after a fish? You English..."

"Welsh. I'm Welsh."

"That must be it." His expression grows somber.

"Must be what?"

"Why I like you."

"Like me? I assumed you just tolerated me."

He blows a French raspberry sound and shakes his head, patting my shoulder as he walks up to the door. "You do make it difficult, my friend, but some of us know a fellow softie no matter how hard he seems from the outside."

Stunned, I watch him enter the code and enter my building, then just manage to slip in behind him before the door slams shut.

CHAPTER SEVENTEEN

*J*ules

I wake up with the kind of dull, thumping head pain that comes from hangovers or heartache.

Or, in this case, a combination of the two.

I don't want to go. But I have to. Starting tomorrow, I'll no longer have a place to stay or a job. And I don't hang around when my time's up. I just don't. I can't. If I do...

No. No, sticking around too long is a trap I'll never fall into again.

Burrowing deeper into my pillow in search of more blessed sleep, I try to visualize Italy right now. Milan for New Years—San Sylvestro. It'll be festive. So much fun.

So, so fun.

With my face screwed up tight from the effort not to cry any more *annoying* tears, I dig deeper into the pillow and then pull the thing out to stuff it over my head and cut out the daylight entirely. The second the pillow's gone, I hear something.

What is that? Music? Please let it not be Colin blaring some angry, rhythmic crap downstairs. I can't take it. I can't take his bitterness when I'm feeling so—

Wait, is that George Michael? No. No way.

I sit up and cock my ear.

Oh my God, it is. And the song is "Last Christmas." I only know it because Nana has always been a fan. Also, everyone I've ever met from the UK considers it to be a cornerstone of the Christmas canon, no matter their age, so I've heard it a *lot* over the years.

Who's playing that?

Someone else must be home. No way is it him. Oh, please tell me Enora's back.

She's got to be home early. Which isn't a good sign for her relationship. Or maybe it is, given how awful I find her boyfriend. A break-up is the best possible scenario.

Relief runs through me at the idea that she's here and I can spill everything that happened last night and she'll laugh when I tell her what we did in the elevator and all the things we said. Well, not all of it. I won't tell her about the personal things he shared. Those are for me. They're mine.

Ours.

I drag my robe on over my silly reindeer PJs, slide into my flip-flops and race to the front door, still convinced that it's her, except the moment I'm on the landing, I understand my error.

Of course it isn't her. I've never heard music from her place. Just from his.

Le Grump's.

Only he's not Le Grump anymore. He's Colin.

And Colin absolutely, positively does not listen to Christmas songs by eighties pop groups. Never. Not once in his life. I guarantee it.

It's that certainty that pushes me heedlessly down the stairs, raises my hand and has me pounding on his door, as if him listening to Christmas music—on the morning in question, no less—is an aberration that I must immediately nip in the bud.

My headache's forgotten, my raw, aching insides along with it. It's not until I hear his footsteps inside that I recognize the absolute oddity of what I'm doing, standing out here, ready to confront him because he's not supposed to like anything holiday-themed or even remotely joyous. I consider running up the stairs as fast as I can, but then he throws open his door and I'm met with—

"Merry Christmas, love."

I blink.

He reaches out and gently grasps my wrist and tugs me inside and everywhere I look, it's Christmas.

"Am I... Is this a dream?"

"What's that?" he leans close, cupping the ear which is currently muffled by a Santa Claus hat and a bright green scarf. Below it, he's wearing the ugliest Holiday sweater I've ever seen over jeans that hug his thighs so lovingly, it occurs to me that I forgot to pay attention to them last night.

The man's a rugby player, for God's sake. He's got the thighs of a Norse god. How, *how* did I forget to drink them in when I had the chance? Maybe I can get him naked one more time. Maybe that would be acceptable, despite the resolution I made not to see him again.

"You all right, love?" he asks, looking worried at the way I'm staring at his bottom half. And then, God, how can I not love him when he asks, "You checking out my big cock again?"

At my embarrassed gasp, he leans in with a smirk. "You can, you know. Anytime you like. I'd be happy to drop trou and—"

"Eh, Colin! Elle est où la creme dessert?" A man walks around the corner—also in a red hat, I note—and comes to a dead stop when he sees me. "Oh, sorry," he continues in French. "Didn't hear the bell."

"I knocked," I reply, too stunned to say anything of substance.

"I'll turn down the music," Colin says, shit-eating grin still in place. "Hold on." He turns to go and then spins back, bends and kisses my cheek, before walking away.

"Salut! I'm Raf," says the man in the hat, smiling wide enough to reveal a few spaces where he once had teeth. "I work downstairs."

"Oh!" I shake the hand he's offered and finally remember where I've seen him. "I bought chestnuts from you! Are you...*roommates*?" I've never seen this man in our building

"Oh, no. I live in the suburbs and missed the last

135

train out." A grinning Raf turns to Colin as he reenters. "You taking her down?"

"Down where?"

"You'll see." Colin glances at me with something that looks like trepidation. Or maybe excitement. I can't tell. This is all so unexpected that my gauges aren't functioning. "You'll need a coat."

"What's going on? Where are we—?"

Colin moves in and takes my hands, leaning down to put his forehead close to mine. "Would you do one thing? With me? For me? Please?"

"What thing?"

"Something happened last night."

"Of course something happened," I say, tired and puffy and swollen from crying and thinking too much. Thinking and thinking as if my mind is a place I actually want to spend time. "Of *course* it did. We got stuck in an elevator and did things and said things and fucking *felt* things that made me think differently about my life and now I've got to go and...*figure out* how to put myself back together the way I was before. The way I *made* myself. In order to..." In my peripheral vision, the other man—Raf—takes a careful step back, like he's trying to tiptoe out of here and I hate, hate, hate that I start to cry right here, in front of him. And Colin. Especially Colin. "To *get by*, Colin. It's how I survive, okay? It's how I've always survived."

"Why? Why do you have to go?"

"*Why?* Because I don't *belong* here."

"Course you do."

"No. No, see that's not how it works. See, every time

I think I've found my place or people or my…a…family, it turns out I'm not what they really wanted. I'm fun, though, you know? I'm good at being fun. I keep it light. And temporary. In and out before things get too…"

"Permanent?"

"Nothing's permanent, Colin." My whisper's harsh, raw, close to angry. "You *know* that."

He nods, his expression so tender that I want to sob into his chest, but that's not what I do when things get hard. It's not. I don't sob or feel sorry for myself, I smile and move on. "I move on, don't you get it? I move on, I don't stay." I find a fresh, clean slate and fill it up and then… "If I stay, I'm afraid I'll…"

"Get hurt again?" he whispers.

Raf totally disappears through the doorway and I want to do the same. I want to duck back out the way I came in and race up the stairs and pack up my stuff and go.

Go, go, go.

Being the one to leave is so much better than rejection. Than being replaced.

"I know," Colin says from way too close. And then closer. "I know, love. I know. I've been the same. Well, different, but the same."

And then his arms are around me and I'm forced to nuzzle into the warm safety of his chest and I resent him for feeling so much like what home should be. So right I can't breathe without smelling it, can't move without touching it. And if I look. If I let myself see past the fear…

"No," I tell him through my sniffles. "I can't stay."

"All right, love. That's alri'."

"Why do you sound like that?"

"Like what?"

"So...so sweet?"

His chest shakes with what's got to be laughter, though how he can see humor here when everything's so terrible, I can't begin to understand.

"Because you reminded me, darling. Of how sweet life can be. How good it is when I let myself live it."

I sniff again and let out the kind of shaky, exhausted breath I don't think I've taken since I was a kid, since before Mom went and died on me, leaving me alone with a father who didn't want me as much as his new kids. "*I* did that?"

"Yeah. Yes, you did. You. And the creepy magic lift, I suppose." Another laugh. "Raf over there, too, actually. All of it. It's a miracle, isn't it, love? A bloody Christmas miracle."

I sniffle again and shake my head and try to press myself into him, to shut my eyes, and return to the darkness that brought us together and, in doing so, showed us the light. At least there, I could see all the things so clearly.

In the bright day, with his smile lighting everything up, I'm not sure I can deny what my heart truly wishes for.

I'm not even sure I want to.

CHAPTER EIGHTEEN

*C*olin

    I walk her up to her flat and wait while she gets into something appropriately festive and when she tries to put on a pair of warm boots by the door, I shake my head and point at the sparkly shoes from last night.

"I believe the absurd torture devices are in order."

"I can't walk far in these," she says, swiping at the red tip of her nose.

"No need. Just a trip downstairs, then—"

"I'm taking the steps."

"Fair enough. Then a quick hop over to the pub. That's all it is."

"Your pub?" Her eyes light up. "I always avoid it, but the fireplace looks so cozy."

My belly tightens. "Well, why the hell did you avoid it, then?" The look she gives me is baleful. And who can blame her? "You're right. The barman can be a right prick."

She rolls her eyes in response and steps into her

shoes, using my shoulder for support. A new warmth curls deep in my belly. I take her coat off a peg and hold it out for her to slip on.

"But the word on the street is that he's turned over a new leaf. Only a prick now on Sundays." I grin. "And to wankers who order a single coffee and park their arses all day."

After she locks up her place, we tromp downstairs at a pace slowed significantly by those razor-thin heels and I don't feel the slightest bit put out by the delay or the sight of her arse swaying in that dress, above those shoes.

There's no rush. She's already mine.

I think those words for possibly the thousandth time today. Or, rather, I *feel* them, in my bones. The way I felt the connection with my brother, when he still lived. The knowledge that we were family. You couldn't break that bond. And, on a good day, like today, perhaps I'll feel it with him again.

This woman is meant to be mine. She just doesn't see it yet.

I stop her before we get to the pub, pull the scarf from my neck, and wrap it around her eyes.

I'm delighted to hear her sweet giggle as I lead her inside and get her seated.

"We're in the pub?" she asks, holding tightly to my arm.

"Yeah. What do you think?"

"Well, I can't see, but..." She tilts her head, listening, sniffing. There's a lot to take in, I know. Christmas carols over the speakers. Mulled wine and pine needles and the scent of a wood fire crackling in the grate. The smile that breaks out on her face cracks something open inside of me.

Once she's fully settled, I let her go and step back. "All right. Take it off."

I watch closely as her eyes open, her mouth drops, her face lights up as it touches on the fairy lights and the tree and the yards and yards of sparkly things covering every square centimeter of the place.

When her face starts to crumple, I move in and take her hand.

"No. No, love. Don't cry." I point back to a stack of signs I've prepared, marker written on cardboard, like that awful scene from that film she loves so much. "Wait until I'm done with these, would you? Then you can let go and have a sob. I'm afraid I'll never finish, otherwise."

She nods and sniffles, not obeying in the slightest. "Okay."

Slowly, with every muscle full of tension, I hold up the first sign and watch closely as she reads it.

I'M A BITTER OLD GRUMP. AND I KNOW IT, it says.

The second she starts to protest, I drop it on the floor, in the process unveiling the next board, which reads: READ TO THE END BEFORE COMMENT-ING, PLEASE.

With the sound of her laugh deep in my bones, I go on.

BUT THANKS TO YOU, I'VE REMEMBERED THAT I'M OTHER THINGS, TOO.

She nods, slow and sure.

I LIKE TO GIVE, TO LAUGH, TO PLAY, AND SHARE.

Her gaze meets mine and holds it.

I'D FORGOT HOW GOOD IT FEELS TO BE ALIVE.

Her soft gaze flicks up to meet mine again and though I know I should look away if I want to make it to the end without some sort of emotional breakdown, I don't want to miss a single reaction.

AND BECAUSE IT'S CHRISTMAS (AND THAT BLOODY FILM SAID SO)

When she bursts into laughter I regret not thinking to record this moment.

I NEED TO SAY THAT, TO ME, YOU ARE MAGIC.

NOT ONLY BEAUTIFUL AND FUNNY, BUT…

JUST THE THING FOR THIS BITTER OLD HEART.

When our eyes meet, I feel the zing, the connection, that emotional cord we shared in the dark last night.

SO, GO IF YOU NEED TO. BUT KNOW THAT I'M HERE. AND I WANT YOU TO STAY.

She's blinking fast, tears streaming down her cheeks. I look down before I lose it myself.

IN ONE SHORT NIGHT, LOVE, YOU GAVE ME BACK MY LIFE.

JUST THINK WHAT WE COULD DO…

IF WE HAD FOREVER.

I drop the last card and wait, my grizzled, grey heart in her hands.

CHAPTER NINETEEN

*J*ules

I'm stunned and a little broken. Very broken, actually. Shattered.

My heart, so tightly contained in my chest for so long, has just burst wide open. I can't control the tears. I don't even try. It would hurt to hold any of this in.

"Come here," I hear him say, through the wave of salt tears. "Come here, love. Come on, darling. Don't bloody cry."

I'm lifted and, without apparent effort, swung into his arms. He takes my seat, cradling me, rocking me.

"I'm…I'm…I'm a mess," I tell him, just so he understands. "And I don't have a place to stay. And and and I gave up my job and—"

"It's all right. It's fine. It's all right, love. We'll figure it out. I'm bloody loaded, aren't I?"

"I can't guarantee that—"

"Nor can I. And that's the beauty, in't it? No guarantees, no promises except that we'll give it a go and see what happens? Do you want that? Do you? If you don't, I'll survive, but if you do—"

"I do! I do, oh my God, I do. So much, but it's scary. What if..." He leaves me? Or dies? "What if we lose whatever this feeling is? Or I hate the way you chew? Or we can't get along for more than a week before things blow up? Or I'm a horrible girlfriend or you're an axe murderer or..."

"Exactly. This is dangerous. As fuck."

"So dangerous." I pause. "What if you stop wanting me?" I imagine Dad and his wife, Mercedes, and the twins they had less than two years after Mom died.

"Or you me?"

"No way."

"You'll get bored and need to move on, or—"

"No way," I tell him, earnest and sure. And then, sensing I need to add some kind of explanation, I push out the words I've denied even to myself all these years. "I'm done running away."

"Yeah?"

"It's not my fault my dad didn't want me. After the accident."

"He *what*?"

"You know how you asked about him? Last night? Well, he was hurting, too. It's just his way of dealing with it was to move on. Completely. He he he replaced mom so fast and then replaced *me*."

"Oh, my sweetheart."

"But it was fine, you know? 'Cause I couldn't stay still anyway. And Nan's always happy to see me, although she's busy with her own life and then it was like, *fun* to just move on to the next place, you know? And meet new people who liked me and I was loud and entertaining and happy and made lots and lots of friends." The realness of what I'm saying hits me, low and hard to the stomach. It hurts, but it's also a relief to get it out. Airing the truth instead of running from it. "I've been running for more than a decade and I don't know how to be still."

"Well, I'll just have to chase you, then, won't I?"

"What about the pub?"

"I lost one person I love, alright? Instead of sitting here stewing for the rest of my life on what could have been or what I should have done, I'm grabbing this fucking reindeer by the horns and holding on. I'm not afraid." He cradles me close. "Or, rather I *am*, but I'm more afraid of not giving it a go, and missing out on this. On you, us. Aren't you?"

I watch him through the haze of tears and what I see is a man who's as lost and lonely as I am, a man who's as broken and who's figured things out the only way he knew how. But all of that is beautiful. His messed up insides, his grumpy facade, the way a scowl's right at home on his face, but a smile looks like someone plastered it on like the ads they paste up on the Métro station walls.

"Okay. Yes. I'll do it. I'll stay in Paris and…"

"That's all. Just stay for now. The rest…"

"We'll play by ear?" I whisper.

Suddenly, his chest heaves, like he'd been holding himself tightly and now we're both letting out so much emotion. "Come here. Give us a kiss."

I strain up and he bends down and our lips touch and it's absolutely electric. Thrilling and warm and reviving.

"Fucking Christ." He pulls away. "It's still here, isn't it? The spark is unbelievable."

"Yeah," I go back in for another kiss, my body shaky and alive. So alive. And so scared. And so ready. So completely, totally ready to give this thing a try, despite the doubts trying to convince me how badly it'll hurt.

Somewhere behind me, the door swings open to the sound of bells jingling. It takes a second for Colin to pull away, muttering something about bloody terrible timing.

"Salut, les amoureux!" says Raf from upstairs, leading a group of people. Some I recognize from the neighborhood, others I don't think I've ever seen.

"I'd better get to work, hadn't I?" Colin says, setting me on my feet as he stands.

"Work?"

He grins. "Christmas party."

"Are you serious?"

He leans in and kisses me again, that feeling zapping right through me the second our lips meet. "Suddenly got lots to celebrate."

More people stream in, calling out hellos in English and French and hauling various offerings inside.

I'm introduced to pub regulars and neighbors and friends who've come from all over Paris. Some stop in and drop off food—bread and chocolates, an actual roast goose, candied chestnuts, a box of cakes. Others pull up a chair and grab a plate and drink and eat.

The pub's warm and bright and smells like spices and wine and woodsmoke. The music coming through the speakers is carols and the kind of big band Christmas songs I've always adored.

Colin spends half his time kissing me and introducing me and the other half pouring out drinks behind the bar. After an hour spent greeting people and getting the food spread out and mingling and just enjoying all the warm mayhem, I head his way.

He watches me, every step, his eyes warm, welcoming, nothing like they'd have been before.

I lean against the bar and ask, "Should I run up and make some eggnog?"

"Not enough for you here, love?" He sweeps a hand around the room with its twinkle lights and piles and piles of food and drink. "Got every bloody thing you could possibly want."

I grin because it's true. I've honestly never seen such an actual feast or, if I'm being honest, felt this kind of warm, easy camaraderie.

"Can I come back there and help you, then?"

He considers. "Yeah. I'd like that. I'd like it a lot."

Once I'm behind the bar, he leans down and whispers, "Can I just kiss you, like whenever I like? Would that be odd?"

"Not odd." I stare at that sweet, soft mouth. "I want that. Badly."

He swoops in and puts his lips to the side of my neck, sending a shiver down my spine. When he comes back up to my ear, he whispers, "I reckon we've got another hour or so before people start heading home to their families or afternoon naps or whatever. And then..."

My heart skips a beat, my eyes go wide. "It'll be just us."

He nods. "You all right with that?"

I think of New Years in Milan and conjure up big parties and new friends. Fresh adventures in a far-off place. Loud and manic.

All of it leaves me cold.

But when I look at Colin and the sweet smile I somehow helped put on his face, I've got nothing but warmth inside. "I'm a little freaked out. I mean, where will I live?"

"My place? I've got two bedrooms. And I'll bet your patisserie people would take you back. You could work here, but—"

"Too much. Too soon," I say. "I barely know you."

He grins. "Are we out of our minds?"

"Yes." It's a wild plan, totally irrational.

"We'll find you a flat of your own, if you'd like. Whatever you want." His eyes narrow. "This means you're staying? At least a while?"

"I'll be illegal."

"Shit."

"Won't be the first time." I force a smile. "Maybe I should leave and come back and then—"

"We'll figure it out. I can think of at least one legal way to get you a carte de séjour."

My eyes go wide. "Are you, like, proposing something right now?"

He laughs and I do the same, giddy and nervous and

as excited as I am scared. By the time we wind down, we're both way too awkward.

"Bit fast, isn't it?"

"How about one step at a time?" I ask. "In case you go back to hating me."

"I never hated you," he growls, low. "Not once. You were just so…"

I hold my breath. "What?"

"*Right.*"

"Right?"

"Like a wish come true. Too perfect to be real."

"I'm not perfect."

"You're perfect for me, Jules." His gaze on mine is so fierce I can feel it to my toes. "Getting stuck with you was the best gift I've ever gotten."

The front door swings open, letting in cold air and a sprinkling of fat snowflakes, along with an old lady carrying a scraggly, brown dog.

"Is that…"

"Bon, is it finished now?" Madame Christen squawks into the quiet between songs. The murmuring ceases as people catch sight of her. "Did those two fools finally see the light?"

For a drawn out moment, everyone stares, their attention slowly moving from us to our elderly neighbor and back. And then, into the silence, Chou-chou the dog gives a joyous bark, Raf yells out "They did!" and the entire pub bursts into laughter and applause.

"Were we that…obvious?" I whisper to Colin under my breath.

"I haven't the faintest."

"You didn't even like me."

"I most definitely do now," he replies, dragging me in for another slow, deep kiss that tingles all the way to the tips of my toes. What feels like hours later, he pulls away and looks across the room at where our neighbor and her dog are holding court at a table. "I reckon we'd do well to stock up on steak for the dog and champagne for the woman. Lest we anger Fate by taking all these gifts for granted."

CHAPTER TWENTY

*C*olin
        Nobody's leaving and it's driving me mad.
There's tinsel and mistletoe and a fucking Christmas
tree and a beautiful woman to unwrap right *there*.
Unfortunately, half the bleeding neighborhood's arrived
and they don't look ready to leave anytime soon.

I open my mouth, on the brink of letting Ebenezer
back out, when Raf comes up to the bar.

"Want me to close up shop?"

I don't usually trust anyone else with my bar. With
anything, really, but...

A giggle rings out from the front of the pub and an
old man I've often seen shuffling in the square below
swings Jules and then twirls her back into his arms and
she's truly the most beautiful sight I've ever seen and
not touching her right now would be a tragedy of epic
proportions.

"Yep." I dig my keys from my pocket and throw them

on the bar. "I'll clean it up tomorrow. Just don't..." Someone whoops. It's Madame Christen, also dancing, only she's doing it on a table that's wobbling dangerously beneath her. "Let anyone die."

"I'll get them out in one piece. No broken hips."

My eyes meet his. "Merci."

"De rien. Maintenant casse-toi!" He points at the door, kicking me out of my own pub. Doesn't bother me in the slightest.

I grab my coat and Jules's and arrive at her side just as the song's ending.

I wrap her up in her coat, grab her arm and pull her out onto the chilly street to the cheers of the gathered crowd. We make it three steps before falling into each other's arms.

"The party's not over," she whispers against my lips.

"Did you want to stay?"

Her eyes are warm, sparkling, lively. I feel caught in their net, lifted by them.

She shakes her head, straining up. Slowly, I lean down and meet her lips in a kiss that's soft and wet and leaves me breathless.

After a long time, she pulls away with a sigh, leans in and rubs her face against my chest. I can't help but kiss the top of her head, which isn't something I remember doing before.

"Let's go for a walk."

I look down at her, all snug in her coat, with those ridiculous shoes on. "Won't your toes get cold?"

"Oh, I stopped feeling them ages ago. Come on. I

want to see the Seine on Christmas." She tugs at my hand. I follow her over the cobblestones. The trees in the Village Saint Paul are strung with fairy lights, the shop windows lit up with them. A very few people hurry past as daylight starts to fade. Already? Where on earth did the time go?

We turn the corner from the Rue d'Ave Maria to the Rue Saint Paul, and cross the nearly deserted Quai des Célestins. Jules drags me to the wall and leans over to stare at the city lit up, the sky pink, all of it caught and reflected in the water's glow. I'd have denied that magic existed until this moment.

"It's beautiful," she sighs.

"It is." I nod, watching how the light shimmers on the water, the rare couples strolling below, the glow from windows across the way, where people eat and drink, laugh, talk. Love each other. Speaking of which… "I could stay here all night."

She leans back to look at me, eyes narrowing at whatever she sees on my face. "Why do I feel a but coming?"

"Oh, do you now? A butt? You into that?"

Her laugh tinkles like bells as she swats at my arm. "Oh, shut up. You know what I mean."

"I do." The smile drops from my face. "But it's cold as a witch's tit out here and I'm worried about your feet."

"Yeah." She turns to give the river one last yearning look and that delay, that one moment, is when I know we'll last forever.

I can't explain it. It's not something my brain gets,

it's a knowledge that slips in and wraps around my heart. It's the bittersweet way she looks at things, so full of joy, but also the sadness of the inevitable goodbye. Even now, in this moment, she feels pulled in two directions. Stay or go. Enjoy this or the next thing.

It's such an odd feeling to step back from this moment and see myself in a week, a month, a decade, and realize that, in the never-ending ebb and flow of life, I could be a constant. A rock.

For her.

It's not a *place* she needs, it's a home.

"We can stay if you want," I tell her, well aware that my insides have shifted in some inexplicable way. "Give you my socks."

"Would you?"

"In a heartbeat."

She blinks up at me, looking stunned, her smile wiped away. "That's…the most romantic thing anyone's ever said to me."

"Well, you haven't seen my socks." I give her a peck on the red tip of her nose, which leads to a kiss that deepens. I tighten my hold and she molds herself to me with that little whimper I already love. We're halfway to spending the bloody night out here when something cold and wet hits my forehead, followed by another light plop on my nose.

I wipe it off and lick into her mouth, which tastes like cinnamon and sugar and—

"Oh my God," she pulls away, looks up, and squeals. "Is it snowing?"

My eyes focus out over the river, where a boat's just chugging by, all lit up and full of couples dancing, then above it, to where the air is studded with a million tiny moving pinpricks of white. It smells like water on wet pavement and…snow. "Looks like it."

"Think it'll stick?"

I shrug. "Got no idea, have I?" A cursory look at the sidewalk shows a wet sheen that'll be murder on those shoes. "Come on. Don't want you slip-sliding all over. Let's get you home and out of those heels, shall we?" We start back across the street, Jules with her head thrown back, her mouth wide open to catch the snowflakes. I tighten my hold on her hand and make sure she doesn't fall, drag her up when she starts to slide, and keep an eye out for other dangers, such as cars or curbs or the ground.

Occasionally, she'll giggle and throw a look my way, sharing a hint of all that delight, and I've never once felt as blessed as I do right at this moment.

She's an angel. I should sing songs to her or twirl her about. I should wrap her up in cotton wool and make sure nothing ever hurts her again.

But no matter what the tale says, you can't reform a real Scrooge in one day. So, when I lean in and tell her what I'm going to do to her, it's got nothing to do with fairies or sunshine or sugar frosting and everything to do with my prick.

"Let's get you home, sweetheart, slip that lovely dress off, and see how those lips look stretched around my cock, shall we?"

When she moans, kicks off her shoes in a rush, and sprints down the cobbled alley towards our building, I decide that I have, indeed, finally met my match.

With a happy sigh, I gather up her absurd little shoes, and follow her home.

CHAPTER TWENTY-ONE

*J*ules

I'm gasping for air by the time we make it to his door. Five flights'll do that, after a race down a bunch of uneven, cobblestoned alleys. And no way was I risking the elevator at this point. Been there, done that, got the hickeys to prove it.

The climb was worth it, though, totally. In a flash, he unlocks and shoves open his door and we stumble inside. By the time he's turned back from locking us in, I've dropped to my knees.

"Fuck me. Are you for real, love?"

"Are you?" I pant, grabbing at his zipper.

It's down, his cock springs free, bobs forward with a weighty thunk, and my lips are on him.

"Oh, fuck, you naughty girl," he says, his voice low and melodious in a way I've never heard it. "Look at that tiny mouth. So fucking adorable."

I can't talk. I might not ever be able to again, actually, if I get any more of him in my mouth, but god, I want to.

His taste has done something to my insides, flipped them around and rearranged them and now I'm writhing on the floor. I'm soaking and I need pressure between my legs and I can't...quite...get it.

I pull back for air, let my eyes take in his monster dick, with its fat, dark, almost red tip, where droplets gather like dew. With a flutter of excitement, I measure his girth with my hand. My fingers don't touch.

He caresses my head and I lean back and meet his lust-clouded gaze. "So?" I ask, flirty and on fire. "How do they look?"

"Look?"

"My lips." I lick him slowly, like a lollipop, watching him the whole time. "Around your cock?"

His erection pulses at my words and, like a switch that's been flipped, his expression goes from dazed and lost to razor sharp, almost mean.

Funny, how after everything's said and done, I love that meanness. In the sack, at least. Or, in this case, on the parquet floor of his apartment.

"I don't know, love. Give us another go, would you?" His hand clenches my hair, just enough to guide, but not hurt. For a few seconds, he watches my face. "This good?"

I nod. "Yeah. Yeah, tighter." I sink my face onto him, as far as I can go, then I hold it and, finally drag myself back. I've teared up, spit's gathered in my mouth. No way can I do this with my mouth alone. It takes both hands the next time I engulf him, with a hint of pressure from his palm. Oh, God, I'm squirming now, trying and trying to get friction on my clit or, hell, any part of me. I think I'll come if we keep at it.

Another dip, slow and tight, then back for a deep inhale and then another and another. I pick up the pace and lose myself in the motion and he goes wild up there, cursing and moaning and grunting like an animal.

"Look at you, all flushed and filthy. Look at you taking it like that, so pretty, so...Aaaaaah, tight. Fuck, I need deeper. I need your cunt, sweet girl. I need to plow you so badly, need your wet, slippery..."

Before I know what he's doing, I'm on my back, the floorboards hard beneath me. I don't care, though. I'm open and pulsing and swollen and all I want is all of him.

And then he's above me, sliding on a condom with record speed and I mutter something about how we need long term birth control if we're going to do this a lot and that definitely pushes him into a fresh wave of overdrive. He rubs himself through my wetness.

"Fuck, baby. Fuck, all this for me." Another slide, another set of filthy-sounding moans from both our mouths and then, "Hold on tight. I'm coming in."

I take him at his word and grab his arm—still clothed in his coat, which will strike me as funny later.

He presses in once. There's little give. Again, just the tip. He pulls out, stares down at what he's doing, then glances up at my face. "It's fucking gorgeous. You're all pink and plump and perfect with that tiny little hole. All for me. I'm fucking hard as goddamn nails and you're taking me."

Slowly, but I am.

Another inch, another, punctuated by his grunts and my gasps and, after our eyes meet and hold, a long, lush, deep kiss that feels like our souls clash and meld and then he's in and I'm…

"Fuck, I'm coming."

He looks up. "Already?"

"It's…you're…"

"Yeah, you feel that? You dirty, dirty girl." He slams inside and all I can do is whimper. "Feel how good it is?"

"Yes," I gasp. "Yes, yes, yes. So good."

He's pumping faster, higher, then shifts his weight onto one hand and presses his other hand low on my abdomen, which no one has ever done before, and—

I'm coming. The feeling's high and sharp, starting in my belly, my pussy, and spreading out, out, wide, wider than me, which isn't possible, but fuck, fuck, fuck…

He puts more pressure on that spot, hitting something inside me and I come harder, somehow, or a second time. I don't know. My eyes roll back and I'm gone.

Lost. Floating. My skin fizzing, my veins popping, sparking.

He pushes inside me once, twice more, and then stays there and jerks with a sound unlike anything I've heard him make, and I wrap my arms around him, and wait it out.

When I come back to the room, I see the lights first, twinkling around the edges of the ceiling. Then, the pain of the floorboards biting into my ass, Colin's weight on my body, the warmth of his breath against my neck.

I tighten my arms and make a happy noise. The kind of sound I'd only ever use for chocolates, usually, or a really good cake. Slowly, he extricates himself from my hold and leans back enough to look at me.

He's beautiful. His eyes are deep and dark, his hair a tousled mess of brown curls, his cheeks flushed pink. He looks messy.

He looks happy.

It's only then that I realize I'm smiling and he's smiling, sharing this feedback loop of joy. He's still inside me and though I'm guessing his knees hurt and I know my back will never be the same again, this is the single happiest moment of my life.

When my eyes cloud with tears, his widen, he leans down and kisses me, once on the lips, on the nose, on the forehead.

"I think I fucking love you, Jules," he whispers, once he's come back up. And that's when I see that he's crying, too. Just a sheen, but I'm guessing it's not something he does often and it feels like a fucking maelstrom of emotion. But in a good way. If that's a thing.

I nod. Not because I don't feel this connection between us, too, but because my vocal cords are on the fritz. The second they're back online, I'll tell him.

"You've come in and brought sunshine and...Will you sleep here? Tonight?"

"Oh, oh, of course."

He nods. "Good. Good, I I can't..."

"What?"

"I can't stand the idea that I'll go to sleep and wake up and in the morning realize it was all a bloody dream."

"It's not."

"No?"

I shake my head. "I feel it, too. The love."

He pushes out a breath like it's been clogged up inside him. "Want me to get off?"

"Probably should. I mean, I'll need usable legs and a back that works if we ever want to do that again."

"All right. I'd better…" Watching me, still, he pulls out and it's a bittersweet parting, punctuated by my moan and a string of curses from under his breath. All the while, his gaze eats up my face. Memorizing me, maybe, the way I am him.

After another kiss, longer this time, he jumps to standing and gives me his hand.

There's a slightly awkward handful of minutes when he gets rid of the condom and I use the restroom and wind up staring at my raccoon-eyed face for way too long. I'm washing the make-up off with hand soap when he knocks.

"Give you something to sleep in?"

"Oh. Yes, please." I open the door and he smiles at me, handing over a red plaid shirt that's long and soft and I will absolutely be stealing forever.

Finally, wrapped in the warm perfection of his shirt, I head out into the living room and he pops out of what I figure must be the kitchen, looking more excited than I've ever seen him.

"Guess what?"

"What?"

"It's stuck."

"What?"

"The snow. It's sticking." He pulls back a dark grey curtain and points down at the cobblestoned courtyard. "It's all white. See?"

"Seriously?" I skip over to the window and look down. His arm wraps around my shoulders and he kisses my head.

"You're a bloody miracle, Jules."

"Me? I don't think so."

"What d'you mean? You saying there's no such thing as magic?"

I shake my head and look up into those eyes again and just *know* that there really, really is. And maybe it's not a holiday thing. Miracles and magic. Probably not. But it is a screeching, last-minute halt on a race I was running alone.

The fact is, this, even if it lasts a few weeks, or, hell, a *day*, is the kind happiness I'd given up on years ago, in the crushed backseat of a tin can car. I never thought…

"There's magic, all right. And miracles." I grin, reach up, and take his face in my hands. "And getting to take your grumpy ass sledding tomorrow, wherever they do that in Paris, is going to be the biggest one yet."

EPILOGUE

*ne Year Later...*
Colin

When your entire relationship is built on a miracle, the challenge is to keep things interesting in the long term. Especially when the woman you love is a world-traveling adventuress who's done it all, seen it all, and got the bloody T-shirt to prove it.

At least she was in a past life.

In this life, she's a local adventuress. A Jane of all trades. The kind of woman you call when you need information. Or help. Or a friend, or advice. Christ, I've never seen someone with so many friends. Clients become friends, random contractors become friends, waiters, chefs, taxi drivers. Even the bloody tax woman is now her friend.

And here's the thing about Jules—she can do, or find, whatever a person needs. Anything and everything, within reason, of course.

"Around the World Concierge service," she answers

the phone, walking beside me. "How many? Did you call the Tour? Montparnasse? Chez Georges? Yeah. I've got it. Give me five minutes." She ends the call and glances at me. "Rooftop dinner. Tonight." She grins. "A last-minute proposal, before they leave Paris for a year."

I tut, smiling to myself and grabbing her free hand as we cross the Pont des Arts toward the Left Bank. "Rooftop views are overrated."

She taps her phone, sending what appear to be twenty-five texts to probably as many different venues. The woman knows her shit.

I stay quiet, happy to walk beside her while she works her magic. Five minutes later, she calls her client back, telling them a text with details is on its way.

"Where'd you put them?"

"Suresnes." She smiles. "Just outside of Paris. Off the beaten path. They can say no one's ever heard of the place. The chef's excited. She loves newlyweds."

"You found a table with a view on Christmas Eve?"

"Yep." She rubs her folded fingers on her chest. "I got skills."

"You're a genius." I bend for a quick kiss, nearly stumbling into a passing woman in the process.

"Hé! Attention! Espèce d'idiot!" The woman is clearly lacking in holiday spirit.

"Désolé!" I call with a grin, adding a heartfelt, "Bonnes fêtes, Madame!" for good measure. It's my way now, spreading cheer to all and sundry.

Jules, laughing, grabs my arm and skips ahead a few steps. "Wait. Where are we going? What are you showing me?" She looks around at the expensive clothing stores and galleries lining the Seine, squinting at the street sign that we turn into. "You know how I feel about surprises."

"You fucking love them."

With a theatrical sigh, she lets me scoop her into my side and lead her down one crooked, narrow street and then another until we reach our destination. It's a small, unobtrusive, but ornate metal door between two shops.

"I know that in the year you've been here—"

"Year and three months."

I grin. "In the fifteen months you've been in Paris, you've learnt every secret there is. But..." I slide a key into the door, reach in and turn on a light to show a straight, short corridor. The walls are made of stone, the floor is paved. At the end is another door and a lift.

The look she gives me is full of a wicked excitement. "What is this?" she asks, her voice laced with awe.

"Come on. I'll show you."

"I was thinking you'd propose tonight. It being our anniversary and all, but we're already married."

"We're PACsed," I reply, though she very well knows this. "Not officially married."

"As good as."

I sniff, leading her to the door at the end of the hall in quiet disagreement. The civil union is a wonderful option, created to give couples the opportunity to be together without the legal ramifications of marriage. But I want more. I want the real thing. I want permanence.

I just hope the idea doesn't frighten her.

"Go on," I tell her, pointing to the lift's call button. "Push it."

She looks as cheeky as a child when she obeys before stepping back to take in the view. She sniffs. "Smells like paint." The lift slides smoothly into view. "Wow. Look at this thing. Is it art deco?"

"It is." I let a little pride into my voice.

"What is this place? Just a door and a hallway with a fancy elevator? This is weird."

"It is, isn't it?" I can't help but grin. "You love weird."

The lift slides fully into view, lit up like a Christmas tree. The interior is gorgeous, the glossy wood entirely refinished, peacock blue velvet insets recently replaced.

"Oh my God, what is this place?" she whispers, stepping inside like Alice through the looking glass. "How did you find this?"

I meet her gaze in the mirror and follow her inside. "I've been looking all year."

"Is this it? Your second pub?"

"Let me show you."

I push the lift's only button—vintage brass polished to a pristine finish—and enjoy the slow, smooth rise, so unlike the one we first kissed in.

At the top, the doors open to reveal a still-unfinished space. Cozy, like my pub, but big enough for two dozen tables with leather armchairs and plush settees. The decor is yet to come. For now, it's been gutted, the place ready and waiting for us to make it ours. I know that Jules will have thoughts on furniture and decor. I can't wait to hear them.

"I was thinking a speakeasy."

"Oh my God, it's perfect. You could call it The Lift!" she gasps, reading my mind.

"The Lift," I agree. "D'you like it?"

"Yes, yes, oh my God, yes! It's so…" She turns, in front of a set of black ironwork French doors leading outside. "Where does this go? Can I open these?"

"Here." I step up and unlock them with my new set of keys, flinging them wide to let in the sounds and smells and sights of the city that brought us together.

Hand in hand, we walk onto the massive terrace. The selling point, for most. Not for me, obviously. What sold me on this place was the lift. But the private rooftop view of the river and the city skyline beyond were a close second.

"It'll be packed all the time."

"I know. I'll have to hire help. I'll be busy."

"*We'll* be busy. Oh my God, I can't wait."

"You like it, then?"

She turns, incredulous. "I freaking love it."

"Yeah? All right. But do you *fucking* love it, darling?"

"Do I…" Her eyes go dark when she catches my meaning—this woman who only curses when I'm balls deep inside her. "I do. I really do."

"All right. Another question." Working hard to keep my breathing even, I sink to one knee—something I'd never imagined myself doing before Jules—pull out the little box I've been carrying for eight months, and open it. "Say you'll marry me, love. Will you? And then let me fuck you in our new lift."

"Our very own private lift," she squeaks, dropping to her knees beside me, her left hand outstretched.

"With an emergency phone that works. Also…" I lean in, slide the ring on, and whisper, "…I can turn the lights off…*and* back on, at will."

Her gasp is big and real and warm. "I want that. All of it."

"The bar? The lift?"

"The husband. I want the husband."

"Thank fuck." Christ, I couldn't relax until she'd said it. "Now." With my ring safely in place, I help her back up to standing, grab the champagne and food-filled cooler I left here this afternoon, and make sure my phone's fully charged, safe in the knowledge that I've installed every security device imaginable. We can get stuck if we want, but we'll always be able to get out. "Let's desecrate our new lift, shall we?"

"I'd like that more than anything in the world."

And the thing is, with Jules, I know beyond a doubt that it's true.

Turn the page to read Jules and Colin's Bonus Epilogue,
Paris, Interrupted

PARIS, INTERRUPTED

BONUS EPILOGUE

CHAPTER ONE

*J*ules

"Hurry up! What are you doing?" I'm all set up on the sofa, snug in a pile of blankets with a big bowl of super buttery popcorn, wearing a skeleton sleep shirt and the low-heeled faux-marabou house slippers Colin got me last Christmas.

"Just mixing your cocktail, my love!" he sings from the kitchen.

"I don't need a cocktail! I need you."

"You're so romantic." His words are muted by the mad rattle of a shaker, followed by the sound of pouring.

"Oh, stop it. Come on. We've got a movie to watch!" I dig deeper into my nest, so happy that Autumn has arrived and, with it, all the cozy closeness of the two of us together.

"My girl and her zombie flicks." He walks out of the kitchen, martini glasses in hand.

"What? I like a little post-apocalyptic angst in my life."

"In your life?"

"Yep. From this distance."

He hands me a frosted martini glass. Balanced atop it is a set of globular, gelatinous objects speared on a fancy glass toothpick. I let out a squeal, only remembering to restrain it so the neighbors don't complain at the very last minute. But come on. Who doesn't love creepy seasonal garnish? "Is that a set of eyeballs bleeding into my cocktail?"

"Why yes it is, my dear. Lychee and blueberry eyeballs."

"Oooooh, I love them! Let me taste." I sip the cocktail, a fresh lychee martini, then chomp down on an eyeball and shimmy with the pleasure of it all. "Oh my god, that's so good!"

"You're adorable. Come here." He takes my glass and sets it carefully on a side table, then leans over and puts his lips to mine. The second we touch, I'm a goner. As usual.

I figure I'll eventually get used to Colin's kisses, but then he opens his eyes and pulls back to look at my face, his expression so full of emotion, it plants a fresh seed of love inside me, and I realize it ain't happening anytime soon. Not this century at least.

I strain up to kiss him again and he deepens it and now I'm a wet, moaning mess, shimmying on the sofa beneath him, helping him get his sweats down and pulling my sleep shorts to the side and cursing while he shoves my nightie up to tweak my breast and leans down to bite and then—god, I *have* to taste his cock, but he won't let me.

"My turn," he mutters as he makes his way down my body, knocks my knees apart, and licks me open with one swipe of his tongue.

"We'll never make it."

"Mmmm?"

"Through a movie. Without doing it."

A low, evil laugh vibrates from his mouth to my pussy.

I've tried to last out the two hours it takes to watch a movie. We both have. We've discussed it and done our best, but then—oh, god, that feels good—some part of will graze some über-sensitive part of me and I'll start squirming and I'll somehow wind up with my face in his lap. And, honestly, when he's hard and so close to my mouth, I've never been able to resist. Then there's the time he patted his thigh and I scooted up and onto him—just to be cozy, no X-rated activity in mind—and halfway through the movie, he murmured something about just the tip and before I knew it, I'd shifted just enough and he was inside me.

I loved every minute of it. Just like now, when I tug at his curls and he climbs back up my body and pushes my legs against my shoulders and just tells me to be a good girl while he has his way with me and we can get right back to watching our very culturally important film.

"Fuck, you're so wet."

"Oh, yeah," I say in my best porn star voice. "And you're so hard." I'm grinning. "So big."

"You'll take it." Oh, okay. No playful interlude today. Today, Colin's feeling dirty and mean. I love this version.

"Do I have t—"

Before I've finished, he takes himself in hand, lines us up, and slides in to the hilt.

I gasp and the twinge in my abdomen.

"Shit. You okay, love?"

When he starts to pull away, I grab a his his arm and keep him against me. "Hold on. Stay."

"You all right?"

"Yeah. I just…" I look at him, a smile pulling at my lips. "You are pretty big. In this position, it's… Phew."

"Should I stop? Change positions?"

"No. No, just…" I shift my hips back the tiniest bit and he shuts his eyes and groans. "Okay. Okay, that's good."

"Yeah?"

I made another move, using him, in a way, to adjust. It's a little in this position, but the friction's good and the way he seems totally unable to handle it is, as always, a huge turn-on.

Under my hand, his ass tightens just a smidge and, "Oh, yeah," I moan. "That's it."

"Slow, then?"

I nod and sigh with his next careful thrust. Another and then another.

"Fuck, Jules. I love you like this."

"Folded in half?"

"Like a little package."

"Sexy."

"Fucking right." He leans back grazes my breast with the back of his knuckles, his expression reverential, and shoves my t-shirt out of the way, hunching down to cover me with his mouth.

I lose all the restraint of a second ago and make way too much noise.

"Shhh, darling, you're screaming," he says with an evil smile.

"I can't…I can't…" *I can't help it,* is what I want to say, but it won't come out, not with how I'm all curved in on myself, being made love to by this man with eyes that go from laughing to wicked in a split second. "I love you," I gasp.

"Oh, my love." He bends and pulls at my lips with his, bites the top one and leans back to watch my body move, zeroing in again on my chest. In the next instant, his eyes go from loving to hungry, from focused to hazy. I live for that moment. The shift between careful and wild. "Oh, fuck, look at the way they bounce."

I half laugh and half choke when he hits that place high and tight inside me, sending me into a fresh rush of pleasure.

"That's it, sweetheart," he forces through gritted teeth. "Clench up around my hard cock. Fuck yes, you're so tight. You'll drag it out of me, won't you?"

He means his come, which in ordinary moments kind of mortifies me, but when we're in the thick of it? Wow. Just wow.

"I'm gonna fill you now. Fill you to the brim with my spunk. Want to see?"

I nod. "Yeah. Do it."

"Squeeze me tighter. Come all over this cock. Do it." On those last two words, he pinches my nipple, then reaches down to rub my clit and then, then, he says, "Show me that little pink arsehole."

"What?"

"Turn around."

Mid thrust, he pulls out, flips me over, with no help from my limp muscles, spreads my cheeks—oh, god— and licks me, straight up and down between them. He's a man obsessed. With me. With my body. With my sounds and my laughter, with our ridiculous inside jokes, with the way I snore. And, from that very first moment we met in the lobby, with my backside.

He stretches me wider now, straightens up and scoots close on his knees, then lines himself up and slowly impales me from behind.

A long "*Oooooooooh*" escapes me as I press my face into the cushions and luxuriate.

After a few steady strokes, he leans forward, tweaks my breasts, then reaches down and plucks at my clit and—

I orgasm. Flying and flying and fizzing, while his pace picks up, his balls slapping hard against my clit, prolonging this pleasure and then, just as he loses that last bit of control, something bangs, loudly.

Oh no. Please, please, please don't be the front door.

CHAPTER TWO

$\mathcal{C}$olin

I've just reached the pinnacle of possibly the best sex I've had in my life—and there's been a lot of the good stuff over the past year and a half—when the door to our flat booms like it's been struck by thunder. Or lightning. Fuck, I don't know. A goddamn missile.

Jules's "Wha's 'at?" is muffled by the pillows.

"Doesn't matter." I drag myself out and then press back inside her, feeling, yet again, like the luckiest man on the planet. "Ignore it."

A few more thrusts, another one of those gorgeous whimpers from my sweet woman, and the sound comes again. Definitely someone pounding on our door, trying to bash the bloody thing in.

How dare they?

I go from ecstasy to absolute rage in a flash, give Jules's back a final caress, and pull out.

"Better be fucking good," I mutter, as I pull up my

joggers, throw a blanket over Jules and stalk to the door. "Quoi?"

"It's the upstairs neighbor," a deep voice rumbles in French.

I look back and catch Jules's eye as she struggles to straighten herself up. "It's him? The ghost?" she stage-whispers. It is odd how the man's been up there for a while, but we've not once seen him. I'm not sure he ever leaves Solène's flat.

Whoever this mystery man is, he's fucking bold coming down here to complain, given the way his stomping shakes the building. "What do you want?" I over enunciate.

"You're too loud. I can't sleep."

"You're sleeping? It's 8pm mate."

"Yes, well, you two need to knock it off."

Suddenly furious, I turn the locks, throw open the doorm and look up...and up... Bloody hell. He's *massive*.

"Fuck me. You're a giant."

"Is that why he's so loud up there?" Jules calls from where she's fighting to extricate herself from the mound of blankets on the sofa.

"I'm loud?" asks the man, who truly is a giant. And not just any giant, a very familiar one. Blimey, it's Erwan Le Roch. I'd know him anywhere.

I'm about to mention that when he ruins everything by opening his mouth and mentioning Jules. Big mistake. "Your woman sounds like she's f—"

"We hear you, too," Jules, finally freed from her sofa nest, shuttles herself between me and the man I'm two seconds from shoving back onto the landing. "You stomp around up there all night. The walls are too thin."

"Yes, well. It would be nice if you could be less—"

"Here." Jules grabs something from a side table and hands it to the big man, stopping him mid-sentence. We all look at the little plastic case, which is tiny in his palm.

"What's this?"

"Earplugs. Never used. I wear them every night." Jules points up towards at the 6th floor flat, and gives him a kind smile. "Insomnia?"

"Yeah. Yeah. Listen. I'm sorry." He steps back and looks up in the direction of Jules's old flat, the place where it all started. "Listen, I'm not alone and it's a little awkward. Hearing you two." Another look up and I could swear his cheeks have gone red. It's a strange thing to watch a six foot eight man blush like that. And not just any man, but one of the toughest and right now most reviled men in the league. Whole thing's a bloody shame. "I've got a roommate now, see... and, with the two of us strangers. Sort of. And you guys, being very..." His brows lower as he attempts to come up with some adjective to describe what is, I'll admit, a very active sex life. "*Excited* about each other, it is..." One massive, battered hand rubs his forehead and...now I feel sorry for the bloke. He seems exhausted. Worn down. It's no wonder, with the beating his career's suddenly taken. "Difficult."

"Oh, no." Jules, as usual, is pure empathy. "I'm so sorry. Hold on. Wait right here." She disappears, off to who knows where. While the pariah of international rugby stands dejected on our doorstep.

"Want to come in, mate?"

"No. No, that's okay. I should…" Another quick glance upstairs tells me where all of his attention is focused. "Get home. Thanks."

"We'll work on the noise issue. My apologies."

"No, I understand." His teeth flash white in what might have been a smile, there and gone in a split-second. "My situation is…not easy."

Now, that I can believe.

"Here." Jules returns with another set of ear plugs, which she presses alongside the other into his hand. "These are for your roommate." Next, she hands him, with an apologetic glance my way, what appear to be half the cookies she baked for me this afternoon.

Fair enough. He looks like he could use a little pick-me-up.

"Oh." He stares down at the cookies, then looks from me to her and back, with a massive sigh. "Thank you." He nods, once. "She'll like these." With a final nod, he heads up, his long legs taking the steps three at a time.

Quietly, I close the door and turn to face a wide-eyed Jules.

"That's Solène's brother," she whispers close to my ear.

"Plays rugby for France."

"I heard that. He seems…"

"A right mess," I finish.

"Solène didn't say anything about him staying in her place. I thought she loaned it to a friend."

"Think that's the roommate, then?"

Her eyes widen. "There's only one bedroom."

"That would explain the awkwardness."

"Sure would."

"Shall we watch the film, then?"

"I don't know. You think we can make it through without…" Clenching her fists, Jules makes a back and forth motion with her hips, her face scrunched up in the worst sort of grimace. Nothing like her real sex face.

I muffle my laughter and pull her into my arms. "No. No, I don't think we can. But we can work on being quiet."

"Want to make it interesting?"

"Interesting?" I follow her into the lounge.

"You know…the quietest person wins…"

"A massage," I propose.

"Yes! Or footrub!"

"Oh, I'm excited," she says, her fingers wiggling with delight. "Let's play."

"Should we start the movie first, or go straight to the…"

"Movie, definitely. I made popcorn, didn't I?"

"That you did." I follow her to the couch, onto which she flops with abandon, hand her the long-forgotten cocktail and turn the telly on from standby, then settle back, pulling her feet onto my lap.

When I start to rub them, I don't think it occurs to my sweet, excited, suck-the-marrow-out-of-life woman, that she's already won. I'll rub her back, her feet, I'll carry her home in the snow. I'll give her everything she could ever want.

In return, I get *her*. What more could I possibly wish for?

Preorder your copy of ***The French Kiss-Off*** *:* www.adrianaanders.com/frenchkiss
Get a release day email: https://www.subscribepage.com/paris

And read on for a sneak peek…

THE FRENCH KISS-OFF

SNEAK PEEK

CHAPTER ONE

$\mathcal{M}$ina

"Voila." The taxi driver pulls up and points at the entrance to an alley. "Faut passer par là."

It takes me a second to understand what he means. "You want me to go in the alley?" I ask in my rusted out French.

"Yes. Yes. The address is down there. You walk now."

Okay. I don't know how they do things in France, but this sounds like an absolutely terrible idea.

"Non," I tell him, folding my arms and settling back into the seat of the car. "I want to go here." I point, hard, at the address on the my phone screen. "Take me here."

Slow, with the sort of patience I imagine must be a requirement to become a Parisian taxi drivers, he says to me, in heavily-accented English. "Zees eez zee address of zhe flat. Een zhere." He gesticulates with both hands. "Village Saint-Paul," he says with pure condescension. "Eez very nice and fancy weez boutique and cafés. You well love it. But you have to walk."

"Walk," I whisper, everything inside me sinking. I'm so *tired*.

It's not that the alley's dark or frightening. Quite the opposite, actually. He's probably right when he says it's fancy. I'd love to check it out if I were, say, wandering through the city on foot. Not fresh-off-the-plane and jet-lagged, lugging half a ton of luggage behind me.

"Allez, allez," the man urges me out, clearly eager to head to his next fare. "In Paree, Madame, we *walk*."

Great. My first exchange with a local is a lecture from a taxi driver telling me to get off my ass and exercise.

I guess there's no point putting it off. I'm here, aren't I? I've made it. End goal: Paris. The rest will sort itself out.

I need to get up, get out, and get on with this thing I've started, no matter how much it scares the crap out of me. I watch blindly as he sets my suitcase and bags onto the sidewalk, accepts my payment, gives me a final, pitying look, and takes off in a stinky cloud of diesel fumes, leaving me alone.

In Paris.

Oh, God. What am I even doing here?

You wanted this, says that little voice inside me. The one that's kept me home all these years, calm and occupied and perfectly fine with the choices I've made. You could just go home.

Home. Home? Where the hell's that, again? Not with mom. Or Candy, my once best friend, and certain not with Trent *fucking* Hanes.

No. No, I *wanted* this. Paris. Lifelong dream. No

more of Trent's excuses. *We'll have the money next years*, or, I told my parents we'd meet them in Myrtle Beach, or Let's save it for the honeymoon.

So what if it doesn't feel like a dream and feels more like running away? Shirking responsibilities. Escaping my real life.

Real life, I remind myself, sucks donkey balls.

A tall, thin young woman in sneakers and skin-tight pants—an actual Parisienne!—stalks up, throws me an angry glance, and mutters under her breath as she's forced to scoot around me and my mountain of belongings to get by.

I turn to take in the narrow street lined on both sides with parked cars and low buildings. This is it.

One at a time, I pick up my bags, slide the backpack on, grasp the handle of my suitcase, and head into the narrow passage the driver told me led to the apartment I'd be calling home for the next few weeks.

This isn't home, the voice chimes in again. *Home's back with Tr—*

"Shut up," I mutter.

A woman pushing a stroller in my direction gives me a startled look and veers sharply away.

I stop, breathing hard, my armpits damp from lugging so much crap over the cobblestones, and look around. I'm in a little square, surrounded by sand- and silt-colored buildings. To one side, there's a bar or cafe with bright red awnings, a few tables scattered in front, the storefront on the other side has spilled out into the courtyard. Racks of clothes, boas, witch hats...

I'm here. I made it.

I want to collapse onto the bumpy road and pass out, but I doubt the people eyeing me from the cafe patio would take kindly to a frumpy, sallow-eyed early middle-age American squatting their square.

Instead, I spin, squinting at the building numbers. I'm close. I can feel it. 50, over there is 52, and there... 54. I've made it.

The last stretch is easy, like sailing after hours of plowing through sludge.

I get to the bright blue door, enter the building's code and...I'm in.

It smells like...perfume. And food. Spices. A little musty. The floor's a blue and white tile mosaic. There's a row of mailboxes with names like Blandel and Christen and Dumont and Llewellyn-Davis and Le Roch.

I pull the key out of my purse, drag my things to the adorable little brass and iron elevator, try to open it, and only then see the *Hors service* sign, scrawled in pencil, on the door.

No. No, no, no.

"Just come *on*," I say. Talking to myself again.

But it helps, I guess, because rather than whine about not being able to get in that tiny cage of an elevator—probably pre-dates the French freaking Can-can anyway—I grab my shit and start climbing.

One. Two. I take a break. Sixth floor. I can make it. Easy peasy.

Or it would be if I went to the gym regularly back home. Or ever.

I'm a little less than halfway up when the handle

wrenches loose from my ancient suitcase's frame and the whole thing teeters for a split second. I catch it before it tumbles to its death far below and stand here, adrenaline firing behind my eyelids for a good minute before I can move again.

I want to go home.

A door opens beside me. Or rather, bursts open, regurgitating a tiny, yapping dog who dances and jumps a full circle around me.

"Bonjour." I pause, searching for additional friendly words, although I'm not sure I'd find them in English, either. On an expelled breath, I finish with the very original, "Chien." Dog.

Good job, Mina. Really eloquent there.

"You are English?" I jump when I realize there's a woman standing in the doorway, watching me, deadpan. She's in her sixties or seventies, compact, and dressed entirely in black, a stark contrast to her chin-length white bob. There's an elegance to her from which even the plaid slippers don't detract.

"American."

Her lips compress as she nods. "You are going up to the, euh, rugby?"

"Uh." I tilt my head back to stare up the center of the spiral stairs and immediately regret it when a wave of nausea hits. "Solène's flat? My friend's place?"

The woman sniffs, eyes sliding over my jeans and T-shirt to my absolute trash heap of a suitcase. I fight the urge to hide it behind me, as if it were unfit for the eyes of others.

"Once you get up, perhaps you should consider putting that valise in the bin."

A humorless smile tugs at my lips. "Yes. Probably." Though I really hope it'll last for the return trip. There's a not extra euro in my budget for frills.

"Well." She folds carelessly elegant arms over her elegant chest, and sniffs. "I can't help you carry it."

"No, Madame." I feel tiny. Like a child. Or an unruly teenager. "I wouldn't expect that." Obviously. From a stranger.

"You just arrived?"

"Yes. Just off the plane."

"Welcome in France," she says, then, in an over-loud falsetto, sings, "Chouchou!" and waits for the dog to race inside before closing her door with a final, curt smile.

I'm sweating buckets by the time I make it up to the sixth floor landing. Unless they fix the elevator, I'll have to take these steps every time I leave the flat. I try to feel happy about that. Yay! Buns of titanium!

Yeah, right. I'll probably end up hunkering down, getting take-out for ever meal, and calling that a vacation.

Except that's not very adventurous at all. And it's not like this is a vacation, is it? Nope. This is one last chance to locate my soul before I wither, grow old, and die. An Eat, Pray, Love, find myself journey that will make Trent regret what he did and, who knows, maybe even reconsider...

No. No way. Not going back, no matter how this trip pans out. I may have given up my pride long ago, but I refuse to give him a single minute more of my life. Either of them.

I make it to the fifth floor. One more flight. I do one more.

It's not until I'm standing confused in front of a door marked with a tiny Llewelyn-Davis sign that I remembered Solène's warning: *In France, we say 6th floor when we actually mean 7th.*

Sadists. Torturers.

No. No, I'm not letting the anger back in. I'm enjoying this trip. It's for *me*.

The last few steps would be torture if I didn't have the prospect of water and coffee and a hot shower at the end. And a bed. A nice, soft, clean bed where I can pass out and wake up next week if I want to.

I turn and look at the two apartments on the landing. This is it. The left-hand one. A plain brown door, burgundy welcome mat, tiny white doorbell. Solène's haven in the center of Paris.

Mine, all mine for the next five weeks.

A place for me to find myself, alone and quiet.

Whatever the hell that even means.

Pulling my now sweat-soaked T-shirt away from where it's sticking to my chest, I suck in a deep breath, turn the key, push the door open, and go stock still.

My suitcase zipper chooses that moment to give up the ghost and yawns open with a splat, regurgitating, amongst other things, a full two weeks' supply of practical cotton granny panties.

There, standing in the middle of Solène's tiny, quaint

kitchen, is an eight-foot-tall, bearded barbarian. And he is buck-ass naked.

Preorder your copy of *The French Kiss-Off :* www. adrianaanders.com/frenchkiss
Get a release day email: https://www.subscribepage. com/paris

ACKNOWLEDGMENTS

There's nothing so exciting or scary as hitting publish on a new book, especially one as close to my heart as this one. I know it doesn't seem like a particularly big step, but as a half-French person for whom Paris is still my happy place, the idea of setting a story there always scared the living daylights out of me. At the same time, it's something I always wanted to do and, these two rascals came to me, I just knew I had to share it.

Michelle Burleson, you have made such a difference in my writing life. I'm so glad you're a part of my team! Thank you!

Thank you to Leeyanne Moore, who sits and writes with me virtually every single day, along with Joanna Bourne and Sofie Couch. You guys keep me going!

Alleyne Dickens, as always, you're there right when I need you. You're the best. Thank you.

To Annika Martin, whose feedback was perfect and whose cheerleader skills are topnotch: We'll always have Paris.

To Jen Prokop, thank you for your edits. They were exactly what this book needed.

As always, Kim Cannon, copy editor extraordinaire, you rock!

To my kiddos, who bear with me through my deadlines and hardly ever interrupt anymore: I love you guys. And no, you may not read my books. And finally, to Le Husband, whose support is never-ending: Merci, love. Je t'aime.

WHAT TO READ NEXT

The Paris, je t'aime Series

The French Kiss-Off - coming 2024!

Camp Haven Series (Previously Kink Camp)

Kink Camp: Hunted

Possession

The Survival Instincts Series

Deep Blue

Whiteout

Uncharted

Love at Last Series

Loving the Secret Billionaire

Loving the Wounded Warrior

Loving the Mountain Man

The Blank Canvas Series

Under Her Skin

By Her Touch

In His Hands

Daddy Crush More available on the Radish Reading App!

ABOUT ADRIANA ANDERS

Adriana Anders is the award-winning author of Romantic Suspense, Contemporary, and Erotic Romance. Her books have received critical acclaim from the New York Times, OprahMag, Entertainment Weekly, Booklist, Bustle, USA Today Happy Ever After, Book Riot, Romantic Times, Publishers' Weekly, and Kirkus, amongst other publications. Today, she resides with her husband and two children on the coast of France, writing the love stories of her heart. Visit Adriana's Website for her current booklist: adrianaanders.com

Sign up to receive news, sales, and exclusive excerpts:
www.adrianaanders.com/newsletter

- BB bookbub.com/profile/adriana-anders
- X x.com/AdrianasBoudoir
- instagram.com/adriana.anders
- pinterest.com/adrianasboudoir
- facebook.com/adrianaandersauthor